THE GUEST AND THE GUARD

VANESSA GRAY BARTAL

DRY CREEK PRESS

Chronologically, this book takes place in the middle of the preceding book, *The Broken and The Brave*. Ribs, the star of that book, shows up as a minor character in this one, during a pause in his own life story.

CHAPTER 1

*F*ound the girl I'm going to marry.

Jones tapped out the email and sent it to his friend, Frog. He missed texting almost as much as he missed the people he usually texted. He had always sent messages as he thought of them, providing his friends a running commentary on his day. But that was impossible now, as it had been the last year. Roaming charges were too expensive. At least he still had email.

Again? Frog returned.

Serious this time, Jones replied.

Have you talked to her yet?

Jones paused. *Working on it.* Perfection couldn't be rushed, especially not when it looked the way his future wife looked. Tall. Blond. Gorgeous.

What color are her eyes? Frog persisted.

They're, Jones began and paused. He hadn't exactly been looking at her eyes. Not that he was some kind of gross, creepy loser who ogled women. It was just that her figure had been so arresting; it was hard to look past it. *Shut up,* he sent instead.

Frog spared him the obvious reply. The guys liked to razz him about his shallow tastes in women, but he'd never seen any of them go for a girl because she had a "good personality." Why should he be any different?

The phone in his office buzzed and he lunged for it. He was and had always been a people person, something that worked out well as a Navy SEAL. Now, tucked away in an office alone, he felt like he was withering, like a plant deprived of sunlight.

"Sir, this is Stuart. You asked me to let you know when Miss Seymour came back."

Yes! "Thank you, Stuart. I'll be there shortly." *Showtime,* Jones thought, standing to check his reflection in the window. Absently, he rubbed a finger over his nose, wishing not for the first time it would work to erase the freckles away. It was hard to be taken seriously as a commando with freckles and a button nose.

Quickly, he made his way from the resort's inner sanctum to the front desk. There was a queue of people waiting to either check in or talk to the clerk about some issue. Jones let his eyes skim over them, assessing for any threat, before allowing them to rest on the true object of his desire: Victoria Seymour. She stood at the front of the line, a smile lighting her beautiful features. She seemed like the kind of woman who smiled often. Jones liked that. Currently she and Stuart were conversing in fluent French. Jones had no idea what they were saying, but he didn't need to in order to appreciate the way her lush mouth formed the words.

"Excuse me, can you help me?"

The voice seemed to be coming from Victoria. Jones stared at her, confused. How could she be speaking French with her mouth and yet English at the same time? He craned his neck, looking around her, and saw another woman hidden from view, this one shorter and plumper.

"No," he said.

"No?" she repeated, annoyed now.

"I don't work the desk," he explained.

"Then why are you at the desk?" she said.

Normally Jones would have had a difficult time not rolling his eyes at her can-I-speak-to-your-manager tone. Six months of working at a hotel had taught him to pick out the difficult people almost on sight. This one would complain about everything, would make the staff's life miserable until her departure. At the moment, however, her hair diverted his attention. Up top, where there should have normally been a calm mane, was instead a giant clump standing on end, clearly matted together by some foreign object.

"Uh," he said.

She gave an impatient sigh. "Gum."

"What?" he said, reluctantly bringing his eyes to her face.

She pointed back to her head. "It's gum. In my hair. I fell asleep on a window and got gum in my hair, so as you can see I'm a bit anxious to check in here." Still annoyed, her eyes darted to Victoria, who was now leaning forward, touching Stuart's forearm with delicate fingers. Stuart, who was usually immune to pretty faces, looked in danger of stroking out and keeling over. Lucky idiot. Gum Lady cleared her throat pointedly, drawing Jones's attention reluctantly back.

"I don't work the desk," he repeated carefully. "You'll have to wait." *Like everybody else,* he mentally added. Gum Lady's lips pressed together. *She's going to ask for the manager in 3, 2, ...*

"At a five star resort with a three thousand a night price tag, waiting in line is unacceptable," she said and crossed her arms over her chest. A couple of people behind her began to murmur their agreement. Jones could see he was going to have to do something about it, but what? He was the head of security for the resort, not front desk management. He left the front, returned to the back, and dragged someone who knew how to do the check in along with him, hand delivering her to Gum Lady with a fake smile.

"There you go, enjoy your stay," he said, wondering if she would catch the subtle sarcasm in his tone. It wouldn't do to be all out hostile, but neither could he tamp down his dislike. Entitled rich people were all the same, in his view. Not that there weren't occasional nice people who stayed at the hotel. It was just that most of them enjoyed treating the resort staff as if they were cockroaches, as if it somehow made them bigger people to belittle the people who were barely making ends meet in order to help them enjoy their frivolous stay at a luxury resort. *Make the money and then get out,* Jones encouraged himself. All of his friends went into further government work after life in the SEALs. Jones was the only one who went into the private sector. The guys liked to give him a hard time about his soft life on the lush tropical isle. The truth was that he worked too much to appreciate it. Running security for such a large resort with so many visitors in a country not his own was turning out to be more challenging than he'd first realized, at least from a bureaucratic point of view. It seemed he spent half his day filling out incident reports and the other half reading reports written by other people. It was mind numbingly tedious, but the pay was amazing, the same as what he'd be making as a surgeon in DC. And his room and board was included, saving him a mint on rent. All he had to do was stick it out a few years and he'd be set financially. Having money would be a nice change from his time in the military when he'd been average, the same as everyone else. And, really, there were a lot of things to love about resort living. He'd met a lot of wonderful people so far, too many to let the rude ones like Gum Lady get to him.

Dismissing her purposely from his mind, he turned and searched for Victoria, ready to make his move, but too late. She was gone. With a sigh, Jones grabbed a bottle of water and returned to his office.

CHAPTER 2

She had already broken protocol by calling attention to herself in a most egregious way. Not that she could help it. It wasn't her fault she leaned on a window and got gum in her hair. Not her fault a resort that prided itself on customer service had a line five people deep. Not her fault the pair of legs and breasts in front of her was using her powers for evil by tying up all available men in the room. *Don't be bitter,* she chided herself. If Carol had the ability to bend men to her whims and soak up all the testosterone in a room, she would probably use it as often as 36D on stilts did. It wasn't French Barbie's fault that Carol leaned more cute than sexy, and that was on a good day, one in which the majority of her hair was not tangled in a mess of someone else's chew toy.

The salon hadn't wanted to take her immediately, another strike against a place that was racking them up like bug bites in summer. It took going to the dark side and becoming Grumpy Guest to once again get her way. She didn't like to do it but—and she couldn't stress this enough—it was a *five star resort.* She knew from a massive amount of experience what that should entail. So far this resort was lacking in all the ways. Carol pulled out her list and added the spa's unhelpful desk clerk to it, along with the exact time the call had taken place. When this was over, she would give the resort an earful they wouldn't forget. And then they would rue; they would all rue. Until then she would pray and hope the stylist was better with gum than she was with good manners.

CHAPTER 3

Jones did his rounds at the same time each evening. If that happened to coincide with the resort's massive buffet, well, that was a happy coincidence. What could he say? He liked good food, another fact his friends incessantly teased him over. Come to think of it, there wasn't much they didn't tease him about. And he wouldn't have it any other way.

He began to rethink his plan when he ran into Gum Lady. Not that he recognized her at first without the gum in her hair. She had apparently gotten that worked out because now it hung limply around her face like a soggy curtain. He thought perhaps it wasn't her usual style because she kept pushing it impatiently from her face. The hair was different, but her expression was the same—cranky, impatient, imperious. What made it worse was that she was using it to stare at the fruit display. Who could find fault with fruit? Gum Lady, apparently.

"Problem, Miss?" he asked, easing up on her right. He expected her to jump. If there was one thing Jones prided himself on, it was his silent feet. But when she turned to him, her expression didn't morph out of its perpetual annoyance. Maybe it couldn't. Maybe she was born that way and had never learned to smile or laugh.

She pushed her hair out of her face before she answered. "No, it's just..." she waved toward the fruit display as if he was supposed to understand the gesture.

"Did the watermelon say something inappropriate to you? Because we take that kind of thing seriously," he said.

She rolled her eyes, reached for a plate, and began loading fruit onto it. And then she turned to him, holding the plate out for his inspection.

Jones stared at it, confused. "Is this some kind of cultural norm where you're from? Because, I'm sorry, I don't think we know each other well enough for me to touch your melon."

She made an impatient little noise and picked up a piece of the fruit. "Look at this. It's four different sizes."

"So?" he drawled.

"So who is running your kitchen? Who cut this fruit, a toddler with a dull butter knife? And what kind of display is this? It looks like someone's Aunt Jenny did a fruit salad for their bridal shower."

Jones glanced at the fruit again. "Looks okay to me."

"Of course it does," Gum Lady said, staring disdainfully at the fruit. Until that moment Jones didn't know it was possible to sneer at fruit. "Clearly no one here was ever in the CIA."

Jones snorted a laugh and quickly wiped his expression. Obviously the woman was out of her mind. He shouldn't find the humor in that. But, really, what did the CIA have to do with fruit? "Know that first-hand, do you? Were you in the CIA?"

Her eyes snapped back on him and narrowed. "I was the top of my class," she said, drawing herself up to her full unimpressive height. If she weren't so repugnant, she'd be cute, he realized. Too bad her personality killed any hope of that. Jones might go for looks on first sight, but a woman had to have the heart to back it up to hold his interest.

"And you cut a lot of fruit during your time there?" he said in the tone of someone dealing with the mentally ill. Maybe she had escaped from somewhere, or maybe she was one of the rich eccentrics he'd been warned about.

"Truckloads," she said.

"Well, I've known a lot of spooks, and they've never mentioned fruit," he said. Now she was the one who was looking at him like he was crazy.

"What is your capacity here?" she asked.

"At the moment I'm fielding fruit complaints. Normally I head up security." If Jones weren't watching her face, he wouldn't have noticed the subtle shift, from annoyance to alarm, as she handed him the plate of fruit and took a step back. "Did you want to file a formal complaint? I could see if I could have this melon fired," he added.

She shook her head, the curtain of hair swinging limply over her eyes. She pushed it away again. Oddly, now that she had so obviously withdrawn, he found he missed her angry banter, proving he must be lonelier and harder up for entertainment than he realized.

"How'd they get the gum out?" he pressed.

"Some kind of oil," she said, grimacing.

"Is that not how they do it in the CIA?" he asked.

She gave him the odd, confused look again. "Our hair never came into play. If it did, you'd be in trouble for sure."

"Obviously," he said, nodding. *Cuckoo, cuckoo.* "Would you like to file a formal fruit complaint?" He held a square of the melon aloft between them.

"No," she said, taking another back step away. He half expected her to bow to him as she eased backwards, keeping him in sight as if he were the dangerous one in this scenario.

"I'll take care of it off the record, then," he said, popping the fruit in his mouth.

Wordlessly, she took another step back, as if attempting to fade from view, and then turned and darted away. Jones watched her go and shook his head. *Rich people.*

He finished his rounds—scoring more fruit, a cookie, and a piece of pie—and then returned to his office to check his messages once more before logging out and closing down for the night. Not that he was ever really off the clock. About once or twice a week he dealt with some sort of "emergency." Clearly the people who used that word to describe an unruly drunk guest had never dealt with an actual emergency. The first time someone roused him from slumber to deal with an "emergency," Jones had come loaded for bear with two guns and a flak vest, only to find that the so-called emergency was a couple having a very loud and very public screaming match. Jones had cajoled them into separating and given the man his own room for the night. The next morning they made up and were canoodling poolside. Not that they didn't have their fair share of petty theft and illicit drug use, because they did. And twice women had filed sexual assault complaints, but those were out of Jones's realm. In those instances he had contacted the local police and let them handle it. The resort had no interest in being part of a cover up when it came to attempted rape.

He was about to close out his email when a message from Ridge popped up. Since his former SEAL team leader and friend wasn't the type for friendly chatting, he first thought Ridge must have been writing to send a picture of the baby. His son was seemingly the only thing besides Maggie that could make him go gaga, but even that seemed like a stretch for the middle of the day. Jones's heart thudded as he reached for the mouse. Was it one of their friends? Had someone died on assignment? That was the sort of dread he'd faced every day since joining up, the high likelihood that someone he cared about might not make it home.

Maggie flagged this because she recognized the name of your island. Looks like trouble might be heading your way. Don't eat so much you can't fasten your Kevlar. LT

Curious now, Jones opened the attached report and read:

A smuggling operation has been detected on the island of Cote de Paix with connections to the Pemuda Pancaslia (PP) gang in Indonesia, threatening to destabilize the entire country after a truce was reached among warring gangs. The country has asked for international help. An operative will be sent under cover shortly.

Huh. A smuggling ring, right here on his peaceful little island. The old adrenaline started to percolate, but he tamped it down. This wasn't his circus; these weren't his monkeys. The local police would handle it, as well as the undercover operative from the CI... He blinked and stared at his screen, reading the missive again. No. It couldn't be, *wouldn't* be Gum Lady. Spooks didn't *say* they were spooks, did they? And why would she waste her time getting so upset about everything at the hotel if she was here as a spy? Unless that was her cover, angry customer. As covers went, it was a good one. She could be notorious but for all the wrong reasons, giving her access anywhere because everyone would likely give her a wide berth. Had the gum in the hair been part of that? Was the salon somehow involved in the smuggling? Was the resort? It chafed him to think that kind of thing might be going on right under his nose. And if Gum Lady had something to do with it, he felt entitled to know.

He would keep a closer eye on her. If she was spying in his hotel, he wanted to know. And maybe, just maybe, she would need a bit of backup. Unconsciously, Jones popped his knuckles and cracked his neck, the standard thing he did before the action was about to start. He'd been out of the game a long time. It would be good to get back in again. *Ready or not, Gum Lady, here I come.*

CHAPTER 4

The next morning Jones couldn't find Gum Lady anywhere. At first he thought maybe it was coincidence she was never where he was, then he realized it was on purpose. He strolled by the pool, taking note of who was binge drinking and would later be a problem. So far he'd clocked three men and one woman to tell the staff to keep tabs on. By now he wasn't expecting to find Gum Lady, so of course he did. If she hadn't flinched, he might have strolled right on by. As it was she was covered head to toe—in fabric, in a hat, in sunglasses. Of *course* she would be that person hiding from the sun in tropical paradise. He didn't let on he saw her at first, as she flinched and tried to shrink even farther into her cover up. It amused him, that flinch. Jones had always been the guy sent in to ease people when he was a SEAL. If his baby face didn't soothe them, his calm happy-go-lucky demeanor did. But now Gum Lady was unnerved, probably the first time in his life he'd ever managed to make anyone uncomfortable. He shouldn't be amused by that, by her, but he was. Especially if she was a spook. They weren't easily unnerved.

He plopped into the empty lounger beside her and put his feet up. "'Sup, Gum Girl."

Her narrow eyed little scowl didn't waver as it zeroed in on his face. "Congratulations, I've never heard another adult human say 'sup before."

"Do you not believe in slang? In your world, does everyone talk like the *True Grit* remake with no contractions?"

"Indubitably, you are correct," she said, enunciating each word carefully. She switched her focus to stare out over the pool, effectively ignoring him.

Jones snorted a laugh, staring at her closed up profile. She was amusing, for a sourpuss. "So, the CIA," he said, repressing another laugh when she flinched.

"Could you not?" she asked, pressing her index finger to her lips in the universal SHHH signal. "Not exactly public information."

"Agreed, and yet you told me."

"Melon-induced delirium," she said. She closed her eyes and rested her head on the back of the chair. "The sun, it's burning my retinas, even through the glasses."

"If you don't like the sun, why come to a tropical paradise?" he mused.

"I don't always get to pick my locale," she said.

"Right, right, because of the CIA," he said.

"For a security guy, you are seriously bad with secret information," she said.

"I could say the same for you," he said. Was she really a spy? She seemed so…ordinary. But those were usually the best ones, everyman types who could blend anywhere. Though she wasn't exactly blending, layered up and hunkered down as she was.

"I honestly don't know what you're talking about. I'm on vacation." One square inch of her ankle was exposed to UV. She leaned forward, hastening to cover it.

"Yes, you seem intensely relaxed," he said. "Like a Chihuahua on uppers."

She turned to scowl at him, applying more zinc to her nose as she spoke. "Why are you badgering me? Do I look like a security risk to you?"

"No." She looked…well, she looked kind of cute with the white stripe down her nose, every skin cell covered under layers of some kind of cloth. Like someone's adorable little granny. "Is there some medical reason you fear the sun? Leprosy, perhaps?"

"I burn, peel, and freckle, not necessarily in that order," she said, hunching farther under her sombrero-sized hat.

"What's wrong with freckles?" he asked. They were a touchy subject for him, since his nose had so many.

"Nothing, if you want to look like you should be perpetually stuck singing, 'All I Want for Christmas Is My Two Front Teeth.'"

"A lot of adults have freckles," he said, tone turning defensive.

"Okay," she said, and now her tone was patronizing.

"There is something seriously wrong with you," he said. He had tried to give her the benefit of the doubt, but she was irredeemable. Who didn't like freckles? Crazy women who criticized fruit and feared sunlight, that's who.

"There is something seriously wrong with this resort," she groused, giving her towel a hard tug. "I ordered a drink fifteen minutes ago. And where is it?"

"I'm not in charge of drink service," he returned grumpily. Jones was not a grumpy person. The fact that he snapped at her was proof positive of the effect she had on people.

"In a resort of this caliber, everyone is in charge of everything. Absolutely no detail is off limits to your attention. If a guest has a need, it's your job to see that it's taken care of."

He squinted at her, annoyed because a little part of him agreed with her. People were paying a fortune to stay in this resort, so much that probably their thoughts should be attended to before they spoke them, like *Minority Report* but without the crime. And, as head of security, Jones was senior management. He should make sure people were happy, entertained, and well taken care of. But he was a trained soldier, a former SEAL. He hadn't left his adventurous life to cater to spoiled adults. And he especially didn't want to try to make her happy, a losing battle at any time. "That's not my job," he belligerently insisted. "And you are not a nice person."

"I am not paid to be nice," she hissed, adjusting her ugly, oversized hat.

It was on the tip of his tongue to retort that she didn't get paid at all, rich and entitled as she was. Then he remembered she might be a spook; she might make even less than he had in the Navy. Maybe this was her one shot at luxury. Maybe he should cut her some slack, give her a break. He eased forward and lowered his voice to a soft whisper, hovering a centimeter from her face. "If you want a daiquiri, princess, get up and get it yourself." Then he yanked off her ugly hat, tossed it onto an empty chair, and stalked away, fuming—at her, at life, and at the sun, which actually *was* so potent it burned his retinas through his glasses, too.

CHAPTER 5

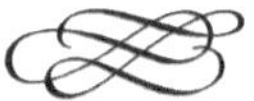

J ones stalked back to his office, ripped aside his chair, and began typing a missive.

LT, what is up with the spooks of the world being universally horrible? (Present company and wife excluded, of course.) I ID'd the one down here, and loathing doesn't begin to describe. SO MUCH HATE!! SO MUCH! Send best advice in dealing before I commit murder.

He fired off the email and felt immediate regret, especially when his former commander took more than a minute to answer. There was a time difference in DC, but that wasn't why Cameron Ridge didn't instantly reply. Jones took a breath and felt the pause for what it was: censure. Jones's emotions had always been too close to the surface, much closer than any of his stoic teammates. The rest of them had been able to carry off difficult missions and keep their hearts intact. Jones had always been the one to blubber if an innocent got in the way. One time his eyes teared up because he accidentally mashed a toad with his diving gear. His teammates called him Kermit for half a year. It had always been Cameron Ridge's job as his commander to keep him in line, and now he did it as a friend, the surrogate big brother Jones had always longed for. Today was no exception.

You okay, Jonesie? Ridge finally replied.

Jones took a breath and held it. Was he okay? For the last year he had avoided asking himself that question because of course he was okay. He was heading up security at an elite resort in tropical paradise. How could he be anything but okay? But with Ridge's question came the introspection he'd been avoiding: maybe he wasn't okay. Maybe he was lonely and bored. Maybe he missed the action of the SEALs. Maybe he missed his family and friends and everything familiar in his home country. Maybe he wanted more than he currently had. Maybe he hated his life.

Fine. Just, you know, spooks, Jones replied.

Spooks get it from both sides these days, lots of pressure. Give 'em a break and try a different approach. If things get too bad, send me a word and I'll see what I can do.

Ridge was pretty high up, as far as spooks went. A senior spy in an elite squad, he had the ear of The Colonel, the highest of the high in their world. Jones imagined Gum Girl getting called back and reamed on his say so and felt a combination of elation and shame. On the one hand, it would feel good to wield that little bit of influence he still held on to. Ridge owed him for a few things. On the other hand, how pathetic was he that he was attempting to use that influence on a girl whose only crime so far had been to criticize fruit and freckles too harshly?

Nah, you know me. Blowing off steam. I'm sure I'll warm up.

I'm sure you will, Ridge agreed and, though Jones couldn't hear his heartening tone, he smiled, reassured as always. *Take care down there. It's about to come to a boil, if the rumors are true.*

Thanks. My love to Maggie, et.al.

Ridge didn't reply, but Jones didn't expect him to. He had always been far more comfortable doling advice than words of endearment. Those were left for Jones, who had no trouble telling the people in his life how much he loved them. He was a people person, good with handling emotion, unlike most soldiers and sailors he knew. With that thought in mind he took another breath. Time to deal with the spook,

Jones style. He was certain that, if he applied himself, he could charm her into a better mood. Failing that, he was fairly certain he could take her in hand-to-hand and hide the body so no one would find it.

Smiling at the thought of getting rid of Gum Girl, he went to find a melon.

CHAPTER 6

Spying wasn't easy. Carol's first job, she botched horribly, had been too noticeable in her observations. They'd made her almost from the moment she arrived. Since then, she'd gotten better at it, much more subversive. But then there'd never been a job like this one.

For one thing, the gum threw her. How was she supposed to be incognito with a giant wad of rubberized sugar stuck to her head? For another, there was the security guy. He'd been suspicious. And then surly, shockingly so. She never should have mentioned her time in the CIA. It wouldn't take too much thinking to put two and two together and figure out why she was here. *Rookie mistake, Carol, rookie mistake,* she chastised herself while she put on a pair of gloves, shoved a flashlight in her mouth, and shimmied under the sink.

When she finished with that task, she sat and made copious notes. Part of her skill at her chosen profession was her attention to detail. Nothing escaped Carol's notice, nothing. It was what made her elite. She elevated being observant to an art form. Her skills were in demand, and she planned to keep them that way.

A knock sounded on her door, and she froze. *I didn't order room service.* She tucked her laptop in her bag and made a surreptitious sweep of her room. Nothing was in view; nothing would give her away.

She opened the door and stood blinking in speechless surprise. The security guy stood on the other side of her door, a tray of melon in hand, uniform and perfectly cubed.

"They're precise, I measured," he said, his tone stuffed with an odd mixture of determination and amusement.

"Thank you," Carol said, taken aback by the strange gesture. "Melon uniformity seems outside your domain."

"We aim to please here at *Omah Kesenengan*." He handed her the tray and rested his shoulder against the jamb. "Did you know that means 'Pleasure House'? Sounds like it should be something else, you know?"

He gave her what was probably supposed to be a disarming smile, but his shrewd eyes gave it away. No doubt about it, he was suspicious. Carol shoved a bite of melon between her lips to avoid answering.

"But of course you probably already knew that," he continued. "Seems like you're the kind of person who does a lot of research and investigation."

"Hmm," she replied, nonchalant.

They squared off, facing each other in silence, only the width of the threshold between them, each hoping the other would break first. Jones was frustrated. He had expected a crack in her frosty demeanor. He was being his most affable and it was having no effect whatsoever. Clearly the problem here was her; she was broken, probably irrevocably. Once again he imagined having her recalled, The Colonel beckoning her back for an epic tongue-lashing. The Colonel owed him, too, in a roundabout way. Jones had helped his daughter with an off-the-books black op that hadn't exactly been legal. Not that Jones would ever call in the favor, but he liked knowing he could. Especially now with Gum Lady staring him down.

Realizing he was the one with all the power in this scenario made him feel better. He took a breath and smiled. Her lashes fluttered in confusion, and his smile widened. "I was thinking. It seems like maybe we got off on the wrong foot. Have supper with me tonight and I'll show you the best the resort has to offer, I promise." He held up his hand as if taking an oath.

To his utter amazement, her face softened into something that resembled a smile. She had a pleasant dimple and he found himself warming, too. She was kind of cute, when he thought about it. Not his type, but like someone's trying-to-be-tough kid sister, plumpish and freckled. Maybe it wouldn't be a dreaded experience to take her to supper. Maybe they could be friends.

She tipped her head, smiling up at him as she made her inspection. "No," she said, and—before he could respond—closed the door firmly in his face.

CHAPTER 7

Carol rested her back against the door and took a breath. What had that been about? Was Security Guy so desperate for answers he was willing to ask her to dinner? Odd. No one had ever been that suspicious before. Too bad she couldn't tell him why she turned him down without revealing herself. Fraternizing was definitely off limits.

Her phone beeped with another reason she'd said no. With a smile, she pulled it out and read the screen.

Hey, Babe. How's it going?

Even after three years together, Carol felt a little thrill whenever she thought of her boyfriend. He was that kind of guy, the kind who made women tingly, herself included. She still almost couldn't believe they were together, even after all this time.

Bah. The worst. Gum in hair. Suspicious security guy. Kill me now.

Aw, sorry, Sweetie. If anyone can handle it, it's you. XO.

XO back at you, she sent, smiling as her thumb swiped lovingly over the phone. *How is it on the coast?*

Cold, wet, windy.

Sounds like heaven. Pretty sure the sun is trying to kill me.

Ha! So come home, he wrote and Carol clutched the phone, blinking in surprise. She had exactly four days off a year, four days when she wasn't heading to some far-flung locale, and she always spent them with him. But home? Did he think of his place as her home? Did she?

Soon, she promised. *Want anything from the tropics?*

A safe return for you. Sounds like bad weather heading your way.

Carol frowned. The last time she checked the weather, the tropical storm was supposed to hit the mainland and barely skirt their island. Had it changed? She'd have to check. Bad weather could wreck havoc on everything. She must have pondered too long because he replied as if the conversation were over, which it undoubtedly was. They were both too busy for long communication.

Stay safe.

XO, she returned, knowing better than to wish him the same in return. Some things weren't safe, and that was okay. Safety, Carol had learned, was vastly overrated.

She tucked her phone away and pulled out her laptop, checking her list. By now she knew exactly what to do and had it memorized, but she always checked the list. Part of what made her excellent at her job was her meticulous attention to detail. She left absolutely nothing to chance.

A knock sounded on the door once again and she stared at it, frowning. *What now?* Surely it couldn't be the security guy again. But it was. Carol yanked open the door and saw him scowling at her. He had the type of face that looked unnatural with a scowl, like someone tipped him upside down, turning the smile into a grimace.

"Have you been standing here all this time, staring at my closed door?" she asked.

"Maybe. Also, shut up."

She pinched the bridge of her nose. "What is your malfunction? Seriously, I have been a lot of places, *a lot,* and I have never encountered this level of unprofessionalism in a security guard before. Is there some type of night school you could go to in order to learn how to do things properly?"

His face, pale at the best of times, highlighting the smattering of freckles over his nose, now turned puce with anger. "That is...you are...who do you think...I am not...I am going to..."

"Should I go away and come back while you try to compose ends to those sentences? Because I kind of have a lot to do," she said, glancing longingly toward the inner sanctum of her room. She was already behind on her work and an inane conversation with him wasn't helping.

The security guy took a deep breath and forced himself to calm. Carol watched him, fascinated. In her experience most men weren't able to regain their composure that quickly. "Look, here's the thing. I know exactly why you're here."

Speaking of colors, she probably paled at having been found out so easily. Obviously she had underestimated him if he found her out so easily. Still, it wasn't within her rights to blow her own cover. She said nothing, regarding him stoically as he waited—with no small amount of frustration—for her to have some reaction.

"Spooks," he muttered, shaking his head. "The point is, I know why you're here, and I want in."

"You want in," she said slowly. "What does that mean?"

His answering smile was cynical. "Keep playing innocent, you're busted. From now on, consider us a team. Where you go, I go."

She glanced pointedly at her watch. "I'm about to go to lunch."

"Excellent, I'm starved." He stepped aside, making a sweeping, courtly gesture with his hand. "After you, milady."

"You are so odd," she said, regarding him intently.

"And you are...well, it's best to keep my opinions to myself, for the sake of community. Never let it be said I'm not a team player."

"You're taking my presence here entirely too personally," she said. "It's just a job."

"Maybe to you, if you're jaded. But to me it's always about people, and a lot people are depending on you, on us. So here we go. Lunch awaits." He nodded his head, letting her know that even though he was being a gentleman and letting her go first, she really had no choice in the matter.

"So odd," she muttered one last time before grabbing her satchel and preceding him down the hallway.

CHAPTER 8

After Gum Lady disappeared behind her closed door, Jones remained staring at it in shock because, somewhat unbelievably, it was the first time anyone had ever closed a door in his face. He was self-aware enough to realize he could sometimes be a pest, maybe to the point of annoyance. But he also knew he was lovable enough to make up for it, that most people considered him the little brother they never had, even people who were younger. He was unassuming, charming, cheerful. Non-threatening to anyone who wasn't an enemy of the state. But Gum Lady, unlikeable, unfriendly, closed off *Gum Lady* was the first to almost nip his nose in her retreating door slam.

Oh, no she didn't. That seemed to be all he could think as he remained staring at her door, slack-jawed with offense. Who exactly did she think she was? Did she think she was better than him because she was in the high and mighty CIA? He could have gone that route, he'd had plenty of offers. He was in the private sector by choice. *By choice!* And it made him no less valuable or competent than she was.

He whipped out his phone and began a furious email to Ridge but halfway through ran out of steam. Not that his anger was spent. He had a ways to go before that would happen. It was merely that he suddenly saw himself from his former Lieutenant's viewpoint.

The positive thing about Jones was that he was a team player. He could always be counted on to get along and ease any tension. He enjoyed peace, cohesion, happiness.

The negative thing about Jones was that he was a team player. He didn't like standing on his own and making the hard calls. It was why he'd never pursued Officer Candidate School. He'd enjoyed kicking back and being a subordinate, as much as any SEAL can kick back. He'd thrived in the high stress world, mostly because he wasn't the one in charge. But he wasn't a SEAL anymore. He was in hotel management now, the head of security. It was time to fight his battles on his own, without Ridge, without The Colonel. And if he couldn't handle one cranky spook, what good was he?

So he made a fist and rapped on the door, so hard his knuckles stung as if he'd taken a swing at it. He made up his mind to pound all night, if he had to, so it came as something of a disappointment when the door was readily yanked open. Gum Lady stood in front of him, her regular pinched and annoyed expression gleaming at him.

And now they were going to lunch together and Jones had never been able to stomach silence for long.

"So. Lunch."

Gum Lady darted him a look, one that ratcheted his annoyance. Why was she so judgy? He could *feel* her censure. She must share the belief that spies were supposed to be severe. Jones didn't agree. It wasn't about temperament, or at least it shouldn't be. It should be about ability, and Jones was able. More than able. He'd been a SEAL, had proved himself in all the ways that mattered. His teammates, men whose lives he'd saved, understood his worth. But on first look he didn't fit the stoic soldier mold. Commandoes weren't cheerful. Jones was.

Gum Lady was not. He wondered if she'd ever cried after a kill. Jones had. Plenty.

"I don't hold out much hope for lunch," Gum Lady muttered, tone longsuffering.

"Why not?" Jones asked.

"Prior experience."

"What has lunch ever done to you? And how could food ever be bad? Food is one of our highest joys in life."

"That's where we agree," she declared.

He grinned. "You're a foodie?"

She gave him the look again, the one that said she had grave doubts about his intelligence. "Obviously."

"Why obviously?" he said, tipping his head to study her. Was she one of those women with a poor self-image who wrongly believed she was fat? She was possibly a little fuller than some, but not unpleasantly so. As far as Jones could tell, all her padding was in the right places.

"Do you want me to lie down so you can make a chalk outline?" she asked, and he realized he'd been caught checking her out. Strangely he felt no shame. Maybe because he found her so unlikeable that he also felt no need to impress her. Whatever the reason, he gave a helpless little shrug.

"If you say 'boys will be boys', I will throw up," she warned him.

"Women do it, too," he said instead. "It's human nature. We look at each other. Nothing wrong with that."

"I don't do it," she said.

"Shocking," he muttered. "Also, you're lying."

"I am not. And why is it shocking? Because I don't view the world as a soulless meat market?"

"Because you consider yourself above it all."

"Above what all?"

"Everything pertaining to us mortals," he said.

Her scowl deepened and so did his smile. He was getting to her. Good. It was his turn.

"Wrong. You are so wrong, I can't even begin to list how wrong you are. You could get a doctorate in wrongness right now. You don't know me. At all, not even a little."

"Oh, but I do. You think you're so superior. You find the flaw in everything."

She blinked, stunned. "That's what I'm paid to do. It's my job."

"But it's not only a job. If you can't find a way to turn it off, you might reconsider your choices."

She bit her lip and glanced away, crossing her arms over her chest. Protectively? Jones decided to make amends. He pointed across the cafeteria. "Sushi. You seem like the type to enjoy it."

"You don't know me," she reminded him with a scowl.

"Tell me I'm wrong," he commanded.

"I…shut up." She pushed past him and headed for the sushi.

By the time Jones loaded his plate and found Gum Lady at her table, she had re-upped her ire.

"Riddle me this, Rent A Cop. If you're so Zen and personally divested from your job, why does my presence here bother you?"

He opened his mouth to answer and found he had none to give. Her presence *was* an annoyance to him, and not merely because of her unlikable demeanor. He had willingly left his former job, had walked away from danger and toward a cake position at a luxury resort. But being confronted with a spook on his home turf was a reminder of all he'd left behind. He wasn't a member of the club anymore, was no longer part of the elite few. Sure, he still had friends and contacts in that world, but it wasn't his world anymore. The reality of that was lonelier and more insecure than he'd expected.

"Because," he said at last.

"Ah, I see. Insightful," she said. Her glance landed on his plate. "Why didn't you get the sushi?"

"Because it's raw fish," he said.

"So you tried it and don't like it," she said.

"I don't have to try it. It's raw fish," he said.

"You insinuated that you're a foodie, and yet you refuse to try food," she said, eyebrow held aloft in what he took to be a challenging manner.

"I don't need to try it. I've fished before, lots of times. I'm familiar with raw fish. No need to ingest it to know how it tastes, thanks."

"Seriously," she said, shaking her head as she picked up a tiny, disgusting green thing, dipped it in sauce, and held out her chopsticks to him.

Jones stared at the chopsticks, uncomprehending. "What?"

"This is the universal symbol for 'put this thing I'm holding to your lips into your mouth.'"

"First of all, you don't seem like the type to share food. Second, no."

"First of all, you don't know me. Sharing food is the highlight of my otherwise dreary existence. Second, open."

He opened his mouth—to protest—and almost gagged when she shoved the piece of sushi inside. Previously he would have said it was impossible to frown and chew at the same time, but somehow he pulled it off.

"Well?" she asked, arching one eyebrow as she awaited his reaction.

"Gag," he said, a lie that became obvious when his glance strayed to the sushi station. Who knew raw fish could taste so good?

"You are a bad, bad liar. Maybe an all around bad person. Who knows?" She shifted her plate of sushi between them and tapped one of the little bowls. "Careful with this, it's wasabi."

"I've had wasabi plenty," he said. "I happen to like hot things."

"You have never had wasabi," she said.

Jones took a deep breath, flexing his fist. He would never hit a woman. Probably. But she was testing his limits in all the ways. "I eat wasabi on my wasabi," he informed her as he speared a piece of sushi and loaded it with wasabi. She watched him, tipping her head in a manner that achieved maximum irritation on his part. *I'll show you*, he thought, shoving the entire piece of sushi into his mouth. Then immediately back out again when it burned like all hellfire on his tongue.

"What is that?" he rasped when he was able, after dunking his tongue in sour cream and downing about half his water.

"That is true Japanese wasabi, nearly impossible to get outside of Asia. Highly unlike the green horseradish served in the US and labeled as wasabi. Hence my warning."

"There is something seriously wrong with you," he said, using his napkin to wipe his streaming eyes.

"No, I'm ridiculously normal and mild-mannered," she argued. "And if you find me so objectionable, stop following me around like a lost lamb. I have a job to do."

"Exactly, and that is why I'm sticking with you. I'm the head of security here. Your job involves me."

"Really, really no," she said, shaking her head.

"Totally, totally yes," he said, nodding.

"In all the years I've been doing this job, I have never been flagged by security, never had anyone insist on tagging along," she said, stabbing her sushi in aggravation, forcing the roll to burst open and spill all over her platter. Then she glared at him as if that were his fault, too.

"I find that hard to believe. If anyone with sense knew what you were up to, he'd want to be involved," he said.

"No one knows," she hissed. "That's kind of the point of my assignment."

"Well, maybe I'm better than they are."

"No, that's definitely not it. It was the gum," she said, turning glum.

"What does gum have to do with it?"

"I blew my cover because of the gum in my hair. And then designer Barbie drew your attention and everything went haywire. Men. I swear."

"How did I get thrown under the bus here? You blew your own cover. Don't blame me."

"I blew my cover because you and the desk clerk were drooling over Miss France's divine perfection. Meanwhile there was a massive backup at check-in and the wad of gum in my hair wasn't getting any less sticky. Hence I blew my cover."

"You say hence too much," he said, pointing his fork accusingly at her face.

"Hence," she said peevishly, resisting the urge to stick out her tongue. How could she have gotten herself in this position? She would have to report on herself, might get dinged, and it was all his fault for not being as stupid as he looked. "This is the worst assignment ever." Angrily, she jabbed her fork into her plate a few more times.

"Hey, don't take it out on the cutlery," he said. He had no idea what made him do it, but he reached for the fork at the exact moment she jabbed it toward her plate, howling in pain when it connected with his hand instead. "What is wrong with you?" he demanded, now staring at the fork as it dangled from his hand.

"Who sticks his hand in front of a moving fork? Are all your instincts backwards?"

"I was trying to disarm you," he said, using his free hand to yank the tines out of his throbbing hand.

"It's a *fork*, not a semiautomatic rifle," she said. "The only victim here was my plastic plate."

"You're clearly violent and deranged," he said.

"Says the man full of fork holes. If this were a cartoon, you'd leak water after you drink now."

He pressed the fingers of his free hand to his temple, not certain he'd ever felt such visceral dislike for a person. "I can't believe you jabbed a fork into my hand and you can't even apologize like a normal person."

"I'm sorry…so sorry you reached your hand between a woman and her food like it's your first day on planet earth," she returned. She gave her tray a little shove and stood. "I am done with this, done with trying to be nice to you."

"Stabbing me is your idea of nice?" he said, incredulous.

She jutted a finger at him. "Stop stalking me. Leave me alone so I can do my job."

"With pleasure. I hope I never see your face again. Or your fork," he called after her retreating back. Several people turned to look at him. He put up his uninjured hand in a wave, giving them a sheepish smile in return. His wounded hand throbbed and he was angry, angrier than he'd ever been at anyone in his life. *No more Mr. Nice Guy,* he thought as he stood and made his way to his office. Gum Lady was going down, once and for all.

CHAPTER 9

I *can't, with her. I just can't.*

She's...she's so...imagine the most punchable person you've ever met and double it.

It's either her or me on this island, and I was here first.

Jones sat staring at his computer a minute before wiping everything and starting over.

Ridge, you've got to get this woman away from me before I murder her.

He erased that also and sat back, sighing. Even though he hadn't sent any iteration of the email, a little of the rage and tension had eased from his too-tight chest. Maybe what he needed was the catharsis of feeling like he had the option to get rid of Gum Lady. Typing the words, unloading on his unsuspecting computer, had felt like a therapy session. She was temporary; he was permanent. He could survive anything for a few days, even an obnoxious little spy.

He spent so long staring at his computer, imagining his hate letter to Ridge, that it felt surreal when his inbox dinged with an email from Ridge. *Did I accidentally send him one?* he wondered, feeling his face fill with heat. Ridge, he knew, would judge him for his inability to deal with Gum Lady. *Grow up, Jones.* He could practically hear his former lieutenant saying it, could feel the censure from a few thousand miles away.

But when he clicked on the email, it wasn't a response to any of his. It was something wholly unexpected, a plea for help.

I was talking to the division head for your region, told him you interacted with his asset. He said there's been no check-in and is concerned there's a problem. I told him you'd make contact and deliver the message about a rendezvous.

The rendezvous was encrypted, using a familiar key, one that acted as a sucker punch of nostalgia to Jones. When he was in the SEALs, they'd developed their own code, using the date Ridge became their lieutenant as the key. It wasn't hacker proof, of course, but it would slow down anyone nosy enough to peek into their private communication. Jones memorized the details and deleted the conversation, then leaned back and stared at his now-blank computer. He thought he was done with Gum Lady, but fate and Cameron Ridge had other ideas. This time, however, everything would be on his terms, and he wouldn't let her get to him. No matter what.

⚷

The best part of every job was the massage. Sometimes the spas themselves weren't up to par, were dirty and not up to code. But the masseuse never lacked in skill. Some things were easy to hide. Dirty equipment was one of those things. But there was no way to hide being bad at touching people, if it was what you did for a living. For that blessed hour, Carol let herself go, let her mind drift and relax. *Heaven, absolute heaven.* At these moments she couldn't believe she got paid for something so incredible. When the job got her down, this was what her mind returned to, the absolute bliss of having all the tension manually worked out of her body.

The room was the perfect warmth and smelled like plumeria. The masseuse applied the perfect amount of pressure in sweet, blessed silence. It was a no-brainer when Carol fell asleep, her head poking through the hole in the massage table like a squirrel staring out of its tree.

"Ahem."

Carol heard the sound from far away but couldn't at first figure out what was wrong with it. *Someone is clearing his throat. Big deal. No reason to wake up.*

"Ahem."

There he goes again. Wait a minute—the masseuse was a woman. Why is a man closed in a small room with me when I'm only wearing a towel?

Abruptly, she sat up, belatedly remembering to grab the towel, too late to cover everything. Whoever her intruder was, he got a good glimpse of absolutely every part of her.

Except maybe he didn't. The security guy stood by the door, hand firmly pressed over his eyes.

"What are you doing?" she hissed.

"Not looking," he said. "Very much not looking. Not a creeper."

"That's debatable. You know how you can tell you're not a creeper? By not showing up in a woman's room when she's getting a massage."

"In my defense, I waited until the massage was over," he said.

"But not until I was dressed and out of the room," she said.

"In my defense, I was afraid you'd get away."

"Stop saying 'in my defense.' There is no defense for this. What is wrong with you? You tell me you never want to see me again and then you show up and see *all* of me."

"I didn't. Seriously, I only saw the towel. And maybe three freckles."

"Oh, my lawsuit," she said, pressing her hand over her mouth. "You are so fired, and this place is so shut down."

"Oh, please. As if you have that kind of power," he said.

"You have no idea what I'm capable of," she said.

"Which brings me to the reason I'm here. Can I drop my hand?"

"No. Absolutely no."

"My arm is getting really tired and you can't possibly still be uncovered." He scissored his fingers, peeking through the opening.

She made an indignant little sound and clutched the towel tighter.

Somehow he took that as agreement and dropped his arm. "See? You're covered. We're all good."

Carol made a slow perusal of the room. "Is this one of those hidden reality shows? Is there some kind of camera set up to capture my reaction? Any minute a producer is going to jump out and tell me I've been set up and the security guy is not actually standing in my massage room, telling me he's comfortable with my level of nudity. It's the only possible explanation."

"I got a message," he said, deciding to ignore her outrage, outrage that had to be feigned. In her line of work, it was imperative to roll with the punches and be comfortable with anything.

"From God?" she asked.

"Close. From The Colonel."

"Does he want you to be an ambassador for his delicious chicken?" she guessed.

He squinted, confused. "What?"

"I don't know. What are you talking about?"

"I have to show you something," he said.

Now it was her turn to press her hand over her eyes. "No, absolutely no. Look, I don't know how you think this goes, but I was not hitting on you earlier. I have no desire to see anything you want to show me in this moment."

Jones bit the inside of his cheek. She was a little funny when she was flustered and, as he'd expected, showing up unannounced in her room gave him the element of surprise. Maybe that was the key to dealing with her, to always keep her off kilter.

"It has to do with the reason you're here."

"To get a massage?"

"Not *here,* here. As in on this assignment."

"What could you possibly have to show me?" she asked.

He sighed, becoming impatient all over again. "Look, could you just please get dressed so we can get out of here and get this over with? I have other things to do." He didn't, actually. But there was no need to tell her that. As far as she was concerned, he was taking time out of his busy schedule to help her, not tagging along on her more important/adventurous assignment like the pathetic hanger on he was now. *I miss being in the game,* he thought. So much that it was worth spending time with her if it meant he got to bask once more in that go-time feeling.

"Oh, I'm so sorry I interrupted your relaxing massage. Oh, wait, I didn't. You can't just come in here and demand I accompany you to an unknown location."

"You know how this goes. These assignments are fluid, they don't always go the way you planned. You get intel and plans change. This is me, telling you the intel is changing. But, being the altruistic person I am, I'm willing to help you."

She was still studying him with the perplexed frown. "Are you telling me you're going to show me something that's going to change my mind about this assignment?"

"Yes," he said, relieved she was finally catching up. She must wake up slowly, an odd thing for a spy who never knew where she might land. But sometimes biology couldn't be helped.

"You promise you didn't see anything when I sat up and the towel slipped."

"Not a thing," he said, maintaining unblinking eye contact until she finally looked away.

"Fine. Go away and let me get dressed, I'll be out in a minute."

He gave a little nod and slipped out the door, leaning against the other side with a smug smile. *I lied bald-faced to a spook and she didn't suspect a thing.* This was one for the record books.

His conscience pinged, and he shoved it away. After all, he hadn't seen *much,* certainly not everything. Just enough to know that Gum Lady wasn't exactly the shapeless blob her layers of clothing and towels previously led him to believe. If he let himself dwell on it, he might admit she had a nicely rounded little figure beneath all the hate and anger. Not that it mattered anyway. When the interior was so unlikeable, it turned out it didn't much matter what was on top. *Turns out I do have standards,* he thought, checking his watch for the time. It wouldn't do to be late, but before he could knock on the door and urge her along, Gum Lady opened it and stepped out, arms crossed over her chest in what could only be a defensive pose.

"I have questions," she said in the same snide tone that was quickly becoming her hallmark.

"Let's walk while we talk. We're on a schedule," he said, turning to march determinedly toward the nearest exit.

CHAPTER 10

"At what point are you going to tell me what this is about?"

Gum Lady waited a miraculous fifteen minutes to speak. In that time Jones ushered her to one of the resort's Jeeps and headed for their rendezvous. She turned her head toward the window, seemingly taken with the view. Not that he could blame her. It was breathtaking, even with the poverty on clear display everywhere outside the resort. It was a strange juxtaposition, abject luxury next to abject destitution. The people who lived on the island fulltime could live for a decade on what visiting tourists paid for one night at the resort. Crime was also rampant. Most visitors didn't leave the resort, unless it was on scheduled excursions to approved locations. Since Jones had been in charge, there hadn't been any security issues with the excursions, but each one was a risk. The locals, many of whom worked at the resort, respected the law and their dependence on the continued success of the resort. But there were others, those who came from the mainland intent on making quick money, who were always a danger. Gangs were rampant. Gangs were what brought Gum Lady here, gangs with international ties that posed more than a localized threat.

"I think you have more intel than I do," he said.

"Are you paid to speak in riddles?" she asked.

"No, but you are," he said, grinning at her.

Her hands tightened on her pack. Like most people who'd lived their lives in high danger situations, Jones had a bug out bag. His was filled with cash, ammo, and extra weapons. He wondered what Gum Lady kept in hers. So far she'd produced a hat and sunglasses, but she'd already told him she viewed those as vital necessities. It comforted him to think she had her own weapons in there. Jones was armed, but somehow it never seemed like enough. He missed the ready access to guns and ammo SEAL life had given him. Now he had a couple of personal weapons, and that was it. If he ever had a fire-fight, he'd be massively outgunned.

"I really don't know how this is supposed to help. I'm supposed to be at the resort," she said.

"That's not what my info said."

"I'm sure not, but that's rather contradictory, isn't it? I mean, I'm here to judge your performance. Of course you want to make it harder for me to do that."

He tossed her a sideways glance. "You're here to judge *my* performance? What does that mean? I'm not part of that world anymore." He was a civilian, thoroughly and completely. Her world had nothing to do with him anymore. Even The Colonel's wrath couldn't affect him here.

"What are you talking about? Of course you are. That's the entire point of this assignment, the entire point of everything," she said.

"What? What do I have to do with anything?"

"Everything. Obviously it's not *only* you, but you're part of it. And clearly someone has tipped you off to keep me distracted. And no wonder. Things are in shambles."

"Hold on. Are you actually saying I'm supposed to be a part of this thing? That your objective from the beginning has been to involve me?"

"It involves everything. Every single detail. I leave no stone unturned," she said with a confidence that bordered on cockiness.

"Okay," Jones drawled. He wondered if she had a screw loose somewhere. Maybe so much time spent in the field had made her a bit deranged. She wasn't talking like any spook he'd ever met. They were confident, sure, but cagey. Speculative. You could never pin them down on an objective. Gum Lady was up front about her intentions, and somehow they involved him.

They drove for a bit to the far side of the island, as far from luxury as they could be while still sharing the same bit of real estate. Jones turned the truck into a dirt lot, bordering a deserted building, and flicked the Jeep's engine off. "This is it."

"This?" she said, studying the building in silence.

"According to my intel, we're supposed to go inside. Lock and load time."

She reached into her bag and withdrew a small tube of lip balm. At first glance he thought maybe it was some high-tech spy gear, but then she opened it and smeared it on her lips. "Ready," she said.

"Okay," he drawled. Apparently she was the calm and collected sort who liked to keep her weapon disguised until she needed it. Jones gave his shoulder holster a reassuring pat, secure in the knowledge that he'd checked it before he left the resort. If things went bad, he was ready, too.

They hopped out of the tall vehicle and walked side by side to the dark building. Gum Lady glanced sharply around, making a detailed inspection as if she planned to put even the landscaping—or lack thereof—in her report.

They entered the dark building side by side. Gum Lady drew out her phone and used a flashlight app to light their way.

"This is…unimpressive in the extreme," she said.

He smiled a bit at that. "I bet you've seen dodgier," he guessed. If she was anything like the other spies he knew, she got sent to some rough and seedy places.

"Not often," she said, cute little upturned nose wrinkled in distaste. Once again Jones thought it was too bad she was so dislikable. Without her off-putting personality as a buffer, he might have been attracted to her. She had a strong girl-next-door vibe he usually found irresistible. Call him a cliché, but he liked clean-cut, wholesome girls, girls he could take home to his mother with no embarrassment.

Growing up he'd watched a lot of TV, mostly reruns from the fifties. Something about those squeaky-clean women sent him over the edge, a fact he had never admitted to his friends, guessing correctly how harshly they would tease him for having a Donna Reid fetish.

They didn't have long to ponder their dilapidated environment. Soon the sound of a rumbling muffler outside alerted them to their company. "Go time," Jones muttered. Gum Lady faced the door, an inquisitive expression on her face.

A man stepped inside then, large and looming and intimidating, backlit only by the sun streaming through the door behind him. Gum Lady clicked off her flashlight app and dropped the phone back into her purse. She might have also reached for her gun, Jones couldn't be sure. He hoped so, though. If there was ever a time for it, this was it. The man before them was supposedly their ally, an informant sent to give them the information about smuggled goods. But that didn't make him trustworthy. He needed to know they wouldn't hesitate to use force, to take him out, if necessary.

"I was told you'd be alone," the man said in heavily accented English.

"The message got mixed up," Jones answered. "I had to deliver her."

The man's eyes moved from Jones to Gum Lady with something like surprise. "This is my contact? This woman?"

Jones looked at Gum Lady, waiting for her to answer. In his experience, she had an answer for everything. She said nothing, however, merely regarded the informant with wide eyes. If he didn't know better, Jones might think she was afraid.

"This is her," Jones said. "We have mutual friends. I was sent to retrieve her when the communication got mixed up."

The man took a step forward. "I do not like last minute changes. It is desperate and dangerous enough without mixups and mishaps. Makes me believe I cannot trust what I have been led to believe."

"The incoming storm has knocked a lot of comms off. Things went a bit haywire. We're golden now," Jones assured him when Gum Lady remained silent.

The man gave one nod of assent. "No more changes or I take back my information."

"So far you've given us nothing," Jones pointed out.

The man scowled. "And neither have you. I demand payment."

Jones didn't think that was part of the original bargain. He glanced at Gum Lady who looked at him in silence, big eyes growing bigger. She swallowed hard, radiating fear and uncertainty. What was wrong with her? Jones had no idea, but she was blowing it big time.

"That wasn't part of our agreement," Jones said.

"It is now. Believe me, when I tell you what I know, you will deem it worthwhile. And I will need something to make it worth my while. It is a death sentence, with no means of escape."

Beside him, Gum Lady was still and silent. Maybe she guessed, correctly, that women's lib hadn't yet entered the equation in this part of the country. Their contact was an alpha male, looking for another alpha male.

"We'll get back with you. But if you don't bring the info next time, we're done," Jones said, refusing to blink when the other man took his measure.

"If you want to make threats, you'd better be ready and willing to back them up. I know I am." His eyes flicked to Gum Lady with menace. Jones refused the urge to place himself in front of her, to intercept that look. She was a professional. She could handle it. He remained silent and alert. Their contact looked between them once more and backed out. Jones waited to take a breath until he heard the hum of his motor drive away.

At last he faced Gum Lady, accusation pulling his features taut. "What was that?" he demanded, facing her.

She regarded him with big eyes, blinking exactly three times. Then her lower lip trembled and she burst into violent, noisy tears.

CHAPTER 11

As if it wasn't enough of a shock to see a trained agent break down into a fit of weeping, she stunned him further by stumbling forward and pressing herself uninvited into his embrace. By instinct his arms came up to clasp her, cuddling her closer like a yowling puppy. Her face nestled into the crook of his neck, wetting it with her tears.

"Shh," he murmured, his hand making soothing passes over her hair.

He waited to speak further until she finally settled, her sobs waning to become little shudders. Eventually she took a step back and used her sleeve to swipe under her eyes. "What happened? PTSD? Did you freeze? What?" What could make a trained operative behave that way, especially one as cool and collected as Gum Lady?

In true Gum Lady fashion, she answered his question with a question, rather three of them. "Why did you bring me here? What was that about? *What is wrong with you?*"

"What? What are you talking about? I intercepted your intel. You haven't checked in. The Colonel is miffed. I was *helping* you."

"How does bringing me to a death den with what could only be a murderer help me in any way? Is this some sort of new excursion the resort is offering? A terror thrill ride to make you appreciate real life?"

"You can drop the act. I have contacts. I know you're CIA. You told me so yourself."

Her lashes worked furiously, spritzing little dewdrops of tears in their haste to clear her eyes. "You must be joking."

"If I am, it's not funny. I don't get what's going on with you."

"The CIA, as in the *Culinary Institute of America*."

The ensuing silence echoed like the aftermath of an atom bomb.

"What?" he rasped after what felt like an eternity. There was no way, absolutely no way anyone in the history of time had ever mistaken the two things for each other. And certainly he wasn't the first to be so monumentally stupid. This had to be some ploy, some spy trick to throw him off track. He licked his lips and stepped forward to grip her biceps, giving her a little shake. "Are you a spy? Tell me the truth. I swear I'll know if you're lying."

"Yes," she said, wrenching free of his grasp and giving him a little shove. His relief was short-lived when she continued. "I'm a corporate spy, sent here to rate the resort. It's what I do. I'm a wringer."

"You...you...you..." At any other time he might be disturbed by that revelation, but not now. Right now it didn't hold a drop of water to his growing horror. "You're a *corporate* spy?"

She nodded. "I go places undercover and rate their services. I thought you knew; I thought you understood the real reason I was here and that was why you've been dogging my steps. But this..." she gestured to the abandoned building. "What even is this? What is going on?"

In answer, he yanked her bag away from her, ripped it open, and stuck his head inside. There had to be a gun in there, *had* to. But there wasn't. His hand emerged from the bag holding a handful of suckers and dog biscuits. "What is this?"

"Anytime I leave the resort I run into hungry children and dogs. So I always bring treats along."

"What about your gun?" he demanded.

"I've never touched a gun in my life. I wouldn't begin to know what to do with one."

So this was what horror felt like, abject horror of his own making. "We have to go now. Right now." Without waiting for a response, he grabbed her hand and practically dragged her behind him, tossing her into the truck and taking off, his heart thudding a million miles a minute. For a while his own panicked breathing was all he could hear, so it came as something of a surprise when he realized she was speaking to him.

"Hey." Finally she jabbed him in the arm, breaking his frantic reverie. "At what point do you get to tell me what's going on?"

He darted her a glance, suddenly seeing her anew. Had she always been so tiny? So breakable? If she was over five feet, it couldn't be by much. And her face was softer than he remembered. Why did he have the vision of her being stern and capable in his mind?

"We'll talk in my office, okay? Let me think a minute." He faced forward again, gripping the wheel. *Your emotions are too close to the surface, Jones.* Ridge had told him that once, the first week on their team. He'd been assessing them all, their strengths and weaknesses. Jones hadn't paid him much heed, truthfully. Mostly because he always saw his ready emotions as an asset. He wasn't a robot like the rest of them, lacking the ability to disconnect his heart from the rest of his body. But now he understood because it wasn't softheartedness that tripped him up; it was anger. Gum Lady had gotten under his skin in a major way and instead of stepping back from the situation and taking a breath, he had rashly assumed she was the contact for whatever current debacle was happening around him. *WhathaveI-donewhathaveIdonewhathaveIdone.* The miserable little refrain played over and over inside his head. Not only had he royally messed up, but he was going to have to fess up to his mistake, both to her and to his former coworkers.

What if I didn't? The thought came unbidden and refused to remain unexamined. What if he didn't call for backup? What if he handled it himself? He was capable, more than. He could send Gum Lady on her way and no one would ever have to know how badly he'd screwed up.

He waited to speak until they were situated in his office and, miraculously, she let him.

"The thing is… See, sometimes in this world…" He paused and clasped his fingers under his chin. "OK, here's the deal…"

He couldn't do it. Once again she looked so innocent and wholesome, a tentative doe standing at the edge of the road, about to be run over.

She rapped her knuckles on his desk. "Excuse me, could I get someone without a babbling speech impediment to give me this explanation?"

And we're back. "That murderous thug thinks you're his contact now."

Her lashes fluttered and then she laughed. Hard. "Oh, my goodness. This is great. Is this some kind of new thing you're trying out? Like Thriller Tourism, right? Because there's definitely a market."

He shook his head slowly and unblinking. Her smile slid to a look of alarm, then fear. "Gum Lady," he began in a conciliatory tone.

"It's Carol," she snapped.

"What?"

"My name. It's Carol."

"Like Christmas Carol?"

"Wow. That's completely new material. In my twenty-seven years on this earth, absolutely no one has made that leap before. You should write for television. Tell me, Paul Blart, what's your name?"

"Jones."

"Are you a supermodel or celebrity? What's the rest of it?"

"Jones will be fine."

She rolled her eyes and snatched a piece of correspondence off his desk, raising her brows at him. "David? David Jones? You're making fun of my name when you're either the lead singer of *The Monkees* or a deceased pirate?"

"It's a family name," he said, yanking the paper out of her grasp. He could only hope it gave her many paper cuts. "Also, shut up." He smoothed the paper on his desk a few times and took a deep breath. "Look, I think I know how we can easily undo this."

"How?"

"You have to go away. Like now. Right now." He clapped his hands together a couple of times. "Chop, chop."

She stared at him with a look that was becoming familiar for all the loathing it held. "Absolutely no."

"Absolutely yes."

"No."

"Yes."

"No."

"Please?" he tried. For a second she paused and he thought the plaintive tone and big eyes worked. Then she scowled.

"No." This time she stood and turned for the door. He dove across the desk and threw himself in front of her, blocking the exit.

"You don't understand. You cannot stay here."

"Why not?"

They were very close now, nose to nose. She smelled like the tropical products the spa used and something else, something sweet, making it harder to say what he needed to say. He sucked a deep breath through his mouth, trying hard to block her scent.

"Because they will kill you."

"No."

"No?"

"No, I mean no. That kind of thing doesn't happen to people. No one goes on assignment and ends up dead."

"Gum La...Carol, I was a Navy SEAL, heavily involved in military intelligence for most of my career. Almost all my friends are still in that track. Believe me when I tell you that you have absolutely no idea what actually goes on in the world. And believe me when I tell you that you are in real and present danger. We have to get you out of this country, the sooner, the better."

"And I am telling you *I can't go.* I am in the middle of a job here. They hired me because I'm willing to go, willing to travel, and I have the expertise and training for the assignment. It's not the kind of job where I can say, 'Whelp, the security guard got me in a pickle so I have to leave the job unfinished.' I will not leave here until my job is done, the end. Find another solution."

"There is no other solution except..." His gaze darted to the far wall. No, he couldn't do it, *wouldn't* do it.

"Except what?"

His thumb pressed the area between his eyes that was quickly becoming a headache. "The only thing left is to call my former team leader and..."

"Are you being paid extra for the dramatic pauses? And what?"

"And tell him how badly I screwed up," he murmured.

"Let me see if I understand what's going on here. You would rather have me cut my job short and leave the country than admit to another person that you, a grown human, made a mistake?"

"You clearly don't know much about men."

She grasped his shirt and gave him a little shake. "Make the call, David."

CHAPTER 12

In the end it went about like Jones thought it would. There were a lot of dreadful silences from Ridge. Jones filled in the blanks for himself. He knew his former team leader well enough to read the unspoken recriminations. *Idiot. Hothead. Emotional. Fool.* Worse than the ominous silence was the final pronouncement.

"I'm sending someone."

"Who?" Jones asked, gripping the phone in a death clutch, but too late. Ridge had hung up.

"You're actually in a flop sweat," Carol noted.

"I'd like to see you deal with Cameron Ridge," he said, dabbing his sweaty forehead. "Actually, I would."

"Why?" She stared at him with wide guileless eyes and he had to remind himself again it was her evilness that got them into this mess. Well, her evilness and his apparent incompetence.

"Because you're you," he said simply.

If possible, her eyes widened even more. They were pretty eyes, he noted. Soft and warm and brown and fringed by thick, albeit stubby, lashes.

"What?" she gasped. "Do you know what my nickname is?"

"No, but I'm going to guess it has the word 'dragon' in there somewhere."

She snorted an indelicate laugh. "It's Sweetie."

"Ironically?" he guessed.

"No. It's because they say I'm the sweetest person they know. Everyone calls me Sweetie, and they always have. My family, kids from school, people from culinary school. No matter where I go, the name follows."

"But you're horrible," he exclaimed and felt chagrined when she laughed.

"Of course I'm not."

"No, you are. Seriously. I like everyone, but I can't stand you."

Far from being offended, she was still smiling like, well, like a Sweetie.

"Has anyone else at the resort complained about me?"

He opened his mouth to say of course and froze, jaw agape. Not one person had said a thing about her, not even a whisper. Usually when they had a problem guest, rumors, warnings, and nicknames flew faster than a hungry mosquito. But no one had made a peep about Gum Lady, about Carol. About *Sweetie.*

"How is that possible?" he croaked. Was he living in a parallel universe?

"I'm quiet, unassuming, and an amazing tipper," she said.

Jones blinked, shocked speechless. "No, that's not right. You're rotten."

She tipped her head. "A minority opinion. And I think we've agreed your judgment can't be trusted when it comes to me, David."

No, he absolutely refused to believe it. When reinforcements arrived, he was certain they'd side with him. Perhaps she hadn't revealed the depths of her loathsome personality to anyone else. Maybe he was simply more discerning than anyone else.

"You're growling," she noted.

"My stomach. It alerts me when it's been fifteen minute past my last meal. I'm like a hobbit that way, in need of constant nourishment." Was he having a stroke? He usually tried to keep his overactive appetite on lockdown until he got to know someone well, a leftover of being an insecure—albeit jolly—fat kid. And now he was word vomiting all over Gum Lady, the ogress.

But instead of using the information against him in some retaliatory way, she smiled. "We have that in common. Come on, let's find food—a talent of mine."

"We have *that* in common," he noted. His friends used to make fun of his nose for food, but he couldn't help it. Somehow he always knew where the treats were.

"You don't know where the good food is," she said, her tone full of the matter of fact certainty he found maddening.

He pinched the bridge of his nose. "Whose resort is it?"

"Migdal Properties."

He opened his eyes, squinting. Of course she would know the name of the conglomerate that owned the hotel. "I meant which of us is more familiar with the resort? Me or you."

"You," she said, poking his pec.

"That's right. So which of us knows where to find the good food?"

She turned her pointer finger away from him and toward herself.

He shook his head, annoyed. She was a constant buzzing in his ears that couldn't be undone now. This was *his* turf, and *he* knew where to find the food. He'd spent the last few months of his employment mapping out the best snacks and the time they appeared on the buffet. Now, for instance, they'd be setting out the chocolate pudding. You couldn't get chocolate pudding at any other buffet time than this one. That was the sort of priceless insider information she should be begging him for. Instead she looked smugly amused as she crooked her ubiquitous pointer finger at him and stated in a ghostly whisper. "Follow me to treats, David."

And then she walked away, not even waiting to see if he'd tag after her. And of course he shouldn't, couldn't, *wouldn't*. She wasn't the boss of him. He'd show her they were playing by his rules now, not hers. She was definitely *not* in charge of him or their destination.

"Where to?" he asked as he slid into the driver's seat of the Jeep and inserted his key in the ignition.

Carol's too-busy pointer finger jutted to the right and Jones swallowed a retort. Wherever she was taking him, it had better be good enough to make up for this injustice.

"Gum Lady, you make me crazy. You really do."

"What? I'm sorry, but it was hard to hear that mini rant over the quaking and gurgling coming from your belly," she said, reaching over to poke him like they were secretly filming a Pillsbury commercial with him as the dough boy. He hated being poked in the tummy. Loathed it, a carryover from his chubby boyhood days. In retribution, he reached across the console and poked her in the same place. And she giggled, mashing both hands over her belly button as she bent forward and chuckled adorably. And it was so cute he almost gagged.

"Now you're just messing with me," he muttered.

"You're hangry," she accused.

In reply, he shot her a dark look. He wanted to rail at her more, but it was true: he was hangry. His cordiality lessoned the farther he was from a meal, and right now he was really far. Too far.

"Here." She held something in her hand like an offering.

"What is it?" he asked, unable to take his eyes off the rutted road to make a full inspection.

"Rat poison. Who cares? It's food. Eat it." She broke off a little piece and shoved it between his lips.

"No, I don't, I can't…" What if he had food allergies? What if he was deathly allergic to nuts or gluten? She didn't even ask before she began stuffing food into him like a reverse Pez dispenser, but maybe that was her goal. Maybe she actually wanted to kill him. The joke was on her, if so. He had zero allergies. But he was picky about certain things—green things, slimy things, germy things, seafood, etc. He had rules. It wasn't okay to go around…

"What is that? It's freaking amazing," he murmured. Birdlike, he opened his mouth for another bite, refusing the urge to smack his lips as she fed him another tasty morsel.

"Some energy bars I take whenever I travel."

"Where did you buy them?"

"I made them," she said, wagging her brows at him when he darted her a look. How could someone so bad make something so good?

Jones faced forward, disturbed. In his experience only the best people were good cooks. He firmly believed food became imbued with every emotion put into it. Negative people made negative food. But Carol's energy bars were sweet and sumptuous, and where was he to go with that?

Maybe my theory is wrong, he mused. But which one? The one that said bad people couldn't make good food? Or the one that said Carol was bad?

Either way, he had the feeling she was going to cause him to rethink everything, and he was in no way ready for that.

"Here," Carol announced, yanking Jones from his deep thoughts. "Where?" he said, eyes scanning the horizon for a restaurant.

"Here, right here," she said, pointing to a man standing beside his motorbike.

"Is he going to take us to the restaurant?" Jones asked.

"Oh, David," she said, again with the inappropriate amusement. Before he could ask her to explain, she had already bolted from the Jeep and was talking to the man and pointing at things.

Jones joined her slowly, wary about what he might find. And it was worse than he thought. The motorbike, as it turned out, was a mini food truck, complete with an array of steamed dishes and sauces that looked as clean as one might expect from a motorbike in the middle of nowhere.

Carol was apparently ordering, saying words as she pointed at things. Motorbike Man smiled happily at her, showing a grin with a lot of gaping, toothless holes that somehow made him look even friendlier and not deranged, as one might imagine. Finally Carol turned her attention to him "And what will you have, David?"

"No, thank you," he said, barely able to choke the words out.

With a sigh, she rolled her eyes before turning to Motorbike Man to point to more things. A minute later he handed them two loaded plates. Carol paid the man, took the plates with a smile, and sank to the stubby, sandy grass beside the Jeep, leaning her back against the vehicle. Jones watched her uncertainly, stomach rumbling in angry protest.

"Sit," she commanded in a bark that made him jump.

"Don't wanna," he said, sounding like a stubborn four year old

"You prefer to eat standing up?" she asked.

"I'm not eating that," he hissed. He darted a glance over his shoulder to make sure Motorbike Chef couldn't hear before sitting down next to her to continue his whisper rant. "Do you understand the kinds of diseases you can get from that? *You literally bought it off a random guy on a street bike.*"

"Do you understand I rate the cleanliness of food for a living?" she asked before popping something into her mouth. She chewed as she studied him, apparently awaiting an actual answer.

"And how can this possibly meet those standards?" he motioned to her drippy, soggy meal. Everything looked mushy, exactly like the sort of food he usually avoided.

"Easily," she said. She loaded a fork of rice something, dipped it in an ugly tan sauce, and held it out to him.

"No, tha…" he started to say, almost choking when she shoved the fork into his open mouth.

His eyes watered indignantly as he chewed.

"You don't know what's good for you," she said, taking another bite from the fork they were apparently sharing.

She was insane. That was the only possible explanation. He must have mis-categorized it at first as having an unlikeable personality. But really, she was straight up crazy. That was the only explanation for everything that had happened.

"So you approve," she noted with the annoying smile, and that was when he realized he had picked up the spare plate and started to demolish it. He paused, staring at it in wonder. How had it gotten into his hands? And how had he eaten so much? And, most importantly, *how was it so amazingly delicious?* Jones hated rice. And mystery food. And hot things. And sour things. He was a meat and potatoes kind of guy, all the way. If he could eat meat, potatoes, and pie every meal for the rest of his life, he would die a happy man.

"What is it?"

"You mean what was it?" she asked as he polished off the remainder of his plate and stared hungrily at hers. "*Siomay*, a steamed pork dumpling with peanut sauce," she used a chopstick to point to the tan glop on his plate. "And chili sauce. Indonesian food is a big melting pot, lots of amazing variety. But of course you know that by now."

"Um, sure," he said, cheeks heating with a blush. No matter what, he would not admit he had taken every meal at the resort since his arrival. And all of them had been some version of American meat and potatoes. But, being Gum Lady, she had some sort of preternatural ability to read him down to his soul.

"David, you have eaten outside the resort, haven't you? Please tell me you've sampled the local cuisine."

"I don't like ethnic food," he said, his scowl as defensive as his tone.

"It's not ethnic if you're living there," she pointed out.

"I don't like rice. Or seafood. Or mushy things. Or hot things."

"Oh, man," she said, shaking her head, her tone turning the words into a near scowl.

"What?" he tried to snap, but it was hard to sound grumpy when his belly was so pleasantly full.

"I thought you were a foodie, like me. Turns out you're stuck on the SAD." She shook her head, eyes rounded with sadness and pity.

"I'm going to regret asking, but what's the SAD?"

"The Standard American Diet. Meat. Starch. Sugar. Processed food."

"What's wrong with any of that?" he exclaimed.

In answer, she shook her head sadly again.

Angry all over again, he pointed his fork at her. "You're condescending. And a food snob."

"A side effect of attending the most prestigious culinary school in the country. Don't you think the US military is the best in the world?"

"Yes, but that's because they are," Jones said.

"Don't you think other soldiers believe the same about their militaries?"

"Yes, but they're wrong," he said.

"Logic is not an apple that grows in everyone's tree," she said. She took another bite of her food while Jones watched, frowning. When she reached the last bite, she loaded her fork and fed him, once again unexpectedly shoveling food into his mouth.

"Why?" he exclaimed, using his sleeve as a makeshift napkin. "Why no warning?"

"Because you'll refuse, and you absolutely should not refuse."

"Carol."

"What?" Her brows lowered defensively, probably in response to his tone.

"I'm still hungry," he said, words turning plaintive.

"David, those are my very favorite words." She stood and put down a hand. "Come on."

He stared at the hand, uncertain. "Where?"

"Doesn't matter. You have no choice."

"Like being back in the navy," he said, but he put his hand out and allowed her to tug him up.

⚷

"Why a soldier?" Carol had found more shady street food Jones otherwise would have avoided at all costs. He was still slightly fearful of becoming deathly ill, but the flavor was so explosively good he was somehow willing to overlook the pending horror.

"Technically I was a sailor. I wanted to protect people, to be one of the good guys," he said.

She studied his profile as he scraped the remnants of something coconut and mango flavored off his plate. "Were you bullied?"

He flinched. It was a long time ago and he was over it, but having someone yank him back to those years of pain with no warning was like ripping off a sticky bandage. "A bit. I was fat. Like, really fat." When she made no reply to that, he thought the conversation was over. Or at least a part of his brain did. Apparently other parts didn't get the memo because he kept talking, long past the point where most people would have been interested. "Being the obligatory fat kid meant I also had to be funny and easygoing. It's the law. So on the surface, I played along. When kids made fun of me, I laughed with them. But inside I was pretty sad."

"Something changed. What was it?" she asked.

"I don't actually know. There was no aha moment. One day it was like, 'That'll do, Pig.' I put down the hoagie and picked up the hand weight. Being disciplined suddenly felt good, so I kept going with it."

"How did other kids react?" she asked.

"Not great, actually. When people have assigned you a role in their minds, it's hard to break out of that cage. They were comfortable with me as the funny fat kid. Seeing me as serious, intent, and ripped must have been a shock. But then school was over. I joined the navy and wanted to keep pushing myself."

"You became a SEAL."

"I became a SEAL. Honestly, I didn't think I'd be able to do it. I mean, I had the drive to change my life, to lose a ton of weight, but would that be enough to see me through BUD/s training?"

"I take it the answer was yes."

He shrugged. "It was a mental game. So was losing weight and getting fit. Not so different, really, when it came down to it."

"Interesting," she said, and she sounded as if she really meant it. Some little hidden part of Jones took a breath and relaxed. He hadn't realized he was defensive about his life until that moment, but he was always waiting for people to judge him, to question him, to doubt him. Her ready acceptance of his life story was a reminder that it was a bigger deal to him than it was to most people, that people didn't see him through a fat kid filter.

"Do you have a girlfriend?" she asked.

He cleared his throat. *Danger, danger, danger.* "Uh, no, I'm, uh, currently between."

She squinted at him. "What is happening right now? What is this?" her hand wove, encompassing him with a swish.

"It's that, you know, we only just met, and…"

"Oh, wow, you seriously did not assume I was hitting on you with that innocent question, did you?"

"No," he lied, letting out a breath that was halfway between relieved and annoyed. Why *wasn't* she hitting on him? He was a catch, even if his mom was the only one to say so.

"I'm making conversation here, trying to get to know you. It's a thing humans do on first acquaintance. And for your information, I *do* have a boyfriend." She fluffed her hair. It was hard not to picture a miffed chicken when she did that. If she gave a loud squawk and laid an egg right now, he would not be a bit surprised. "Why are you smiling?"

He shrugged. "How did you get in the judgmental travel business?"

She faced forward with a little huff, consciously letting go of her annoyance. "I wanted to be a chef, preferably at somewhere like your fancy resort, maybe on a cruise. I wanted to go to some far-flung location and make it. But I didn't have all the necessary components to be a chef, not of the caliber I wanted to be. For a while I worked on some food lines, but it was hard being a grunt. This opportunity came up and seemed too good not to take. The schedule is insane, but so is the pay. And I get to see the world, to stay at the finest resorts, to pretend to be one of the beautiful people for a bit."

He felt like she purposely edited the story, that there were gaps she left out to keep it impersonal. But he was okay with that. For the next little while, she was the job. It was never a good idea to get too attached to the job. Which made his next question nonsensical. "How long have you and the boyfriend been together?"

"Three years."

His eyes bugged. Three years? That was two years and ten months longer than he'd ever been in a relationship. "Are you engaged? You must be by now."

"No," she said. Her wayward stare told him it was a tender topic, one best left unpoked.

"Why not?"

"We don't see each other that often, but it works for us. We both like our independence."

"That sounds like one of those things women say when their man's a cheater," he said.

She wrinkled her cute little nose at him. She had a kind of pug nose, turned up on the end a bit. With the big eyes, freckles, and diminutive size, she could definitely inhabit Whoville. He wondered, but didn't ask, if anyone had ever called her Cindy Lou Who.

"He's not a cheater. He's a great guy, an amazing guy. But he's busy and life is busy." She shrugged. *What are you going to do?*

"I can't imagine dating someone for three years without making a commitment. Just saying."

"My condolences to your girlfriend. Oh, wait, you don't have one."

"I'm between," he snapped. His lack of girlfriend was a sore spot.

She snorted. "I'll bet you are."

"What's that supposed to mean?"

She paused and faced him. He did the same. People began to walk around them, as if they were a new boulder in the stream of humanity now crowding the street. Jones took her arm and shepherded her out of the way, off to the side. "That first day, when you practically tripped over your tongue to get to the desk, you were coming to see French Barbie, right?"

"So?"

She shook her head, sighing in exasperation. "Ridiculous."

"What? That I found her attractive? Alert the media, guy wants to ogle hot girl. Film at eleven."

"No, it's that you in any way believe that's the sort of woman you should go for." She shook her head again.

"Because she's out of my league?" now he was really becoming irritated. How much of an ogre did she think he was? He patted his stomach, reassured by the abs beneath his fingertips. Maybe he'd slacked off his training a little since he moved to the resort, but he wasn't fat again. He *wasn't.*

"It's not about that. It's like," she paused and took a breath, thinking. "Like everyone is in an Olympic size swimming pool, the kind where the lanes are all roped off. We're all the same, all at the same skill level and in the same depth of water. But we have our lanes and we can't stray from them. You have to stay in your lane."

"And you think that woman was in another lane?" he asked.

She nodded. "Definitely. And not because she's better than you, and not even because she's tall and perfect, but because those things have made her who she is. Her life has likely been more privileged than yours, the way it always is for beautiful people. It's shaped her in different ways. Unfair, but true. You need to find someone in your lane, someone who has been shaped by a painful past the way you were. Someone who understands without being told."

He stared at her, blinking in surprise by how much sense it all made. In the past when people had tried to tell him women were out of his league, he took it to heart, as if it was a slam against him, as if he wasn't good enough. But put the way Carol put it, they weren't different because one of them was better and one was worse. They were different because *they were different.* It was so fundamental, yet so profound.

"Huh," he said.

"That girl who brought us pie," she said, apropos of nothing.

"Lucinda?" Lucinda worked for the restaurant; she was his pastry connection.

"Yes, her. She likes you. You should ask her out."

"Lucinda?" Lucinda was cute, but the zing wasn't there. Wasn't the zing supposed to be there? "I'm not sure I'm attracted to her."

"Attraction isn't always immediate. Sometimes it grows; sometimes it has to be cultivated. You know the greatest predictor of finding love is proximity. We fall for the people already in our world, people we see and know. Getting to know someone, spending time with them, is truly the best way to find lifelong love."

"Is that how it happened with you and your part-time boyfriend?

Proximity." He clasped his hands under his chin and fluttered his lashes.

"Sort of. I met him in culinary school. He's my good friend's older brother. I thought he was the handsomest man I ever saw. He has those kind of rugged good looks. Cop good looks."

"He's a cop?"

She nodded. "In Maine. So you see, he's kind of tied down to his job and unable to follow me around the world."

"And you're not ready to settle down in Maine," he guessed.

"I'm more ready than I used to be," she said, doing the thousand-yard stare again. And once again he sensed pain and sadness behind her words. And once again he refused to ask her about them. He told himself he was giving her privacy, but the truth was that he was afraid of the growing friendship between them. Something about Carol loosened his tongue and his reserve. He'd been more candid with her than he'd been with most people in his life. Even his SEAL buddies didn't know the depth of pain his fat kid past caused him. He'd so badly wanted to be one of them—as tough, as indestructible. Admitting he used to drown his pain in a gallon of ice cream would have undone that. But somehow he knew Carol wouldn't judge him, if he told her that information.

Because she's in your lane, he realized. Whatever trauma or pain occurred in her past, it was comparable to his. It had defined her; it had made them the same.

"What?" she asked, patting her hair self-consciously, making him realize he was staring at her.

The way her lashes fanned over her warm brown eyes reminded him of his favorite cow on his grandparents' farm. He'd loved that cow. But telling a woman she reminded him of a bovine was a step too far past stupidity, even for him. "Nothing. You've got me thinking things."

"Sorry," she said, giving him an apologetic smile. "You know what stops thoughts and feelings?"

"Food?" he guessed.

"It's like you're reading my mind. Come on, I saw a guy who makes cotton candy into animal shapes." She took his hand and began tugging him forward. Jones turned off his brain and trotted behind her, happy to snuff out his disconcerting mental chatter. If he wasn't careful, he'd convince himself he was falling for *her*, and wouldn't that be a disaster?

CHAPTER 14

"I am stuffed," Carol complained, pressing her hand to her belly.

"Me, too. It's the best," Jones agreed, and they high fived. Despite the amount of food he'd eaten, it hadn't been bad food, not in the usual sense. Lots of rice, veggies, and fresh fruit. His pancreas probably had no idea what to do with all the vitamins, minerals, and lack of red meat. "I don't even know what I ate today."

"It's probably best that way," she said.

He white-knuckled the steering wheel, suddenly apprehensive. "What did you feed me, Carol?"

"Nothing too out there, no monkey brains or civet. But there may have been some squid and octopus."

"I think I might throw up," he said, stomach tossing violently.

"You didn't complain when you were eating it," she said.

"That's because I didn't know," he said.

"That makes no logical sense, David. You are fine. You were fine when you were eating it, and you're fine now. And you'll be fine later. You need to chill."

"I need to chill? *I* need to chill? That's rich, coming from the most uptight person I have ever met."

"Me?" She pointed to her chest. "I am not uptight. I'm the most laid back person in the universe. Everyone says so. Hence the nickname."

"I haven't heard one person use your nickname. I only have your word for it that it's even real. And so far the evidence is seriously out of reach," he said.

She pulled out her phone and used her thumb to scroll her messages, facing it toward him so he could see, if he was inclined to take his eyes off the road, which he was not. Instead, she read out loud. "Sweetie, call me when you get this. Sweetie, hope you're having fun on your latest adventure! Sweetie, message me about Christmas, trying to plan early this year. Sweetie, how do you make those cookies with the cashews? Those are from four different people."

"Nope, no way," he said, stubbornly shaking his head. "Also, how *do* you make those cookies with the cashews? Because I love me some cashews."

"Sorry, I can only tell people who don't insult me every time they open their squid-eating mouths."

"Carol," he said, pressing his hand to his gut with renewed horror. Squid. He'd eaten *squid*. What was she doing to him?

Of course she laughed at his misery, glancing out the back window with a smile. "Well, that's a big SUV."

"Ha, good one," he said.

"Why is that a good one?" she asked.

"Because no one on the island has an SUV, no one but..." The sound of a loud muffler grew closer. Jones turned to look out his window and came face to face with what could only be a gang member. Not only were they the only ones with access to such expensive cars, but this one was currently pointing a gun directly into his face.

"Well, that's not good," Carol muttered, and if his brain wasn't busy calculating twenty possible outcomes for their current scenario, Jones would have laughed. As it was, he slammed the brakes and did a 360 in the middle of the road, a bootleg maneuver he learned in defensive driving 101. The SUV streamed past, came to its own belated halt, and made a wide, swinging U-turn, sideswiping two other cars off the road.

By this time Jones had a good lead, but the powerful SUV began to gain on them, enough to fire off a few shots that had passersby screaming and ducking for cover.

"Do you want me to shoot at them?" Carol asked, gripping her hands tightly together in anxiety as she ducked low in the seat.

"Do you actually know how to shoot?" Jones asked.

"Of course not, David," she said reasonably.

"Then no, Carol, I do not want you to touch a firearm," Jones said, making a late turn onto a side road that would hopefully get them out of the crowd. It would be more dangerous for them, but less so for the multitudes of people on the street, some of them children.

"You're a gun snob," she accused, gripping the car door as he careened around a corner, tires squealing.

"Let me guide us unharmed through this current crisis, using the skills I spent a decade honing, and then you can ream me," he said.

"I'm just saying," she said. "You can catch more flies with honey than with vinegar."

"You can't catch any flies if you're dead," he replied.

"You don't always have to have a retort for everything."

"Not now, Carol," he said, teeth gritted in annoyance. The Jeep's tires squealed as he took another corner going fifty. If they were in a cartoon, he would be on two wheels right now. As it was, it took every ounce of strength and skill to maintain control of the vehicle. One wrong move and they would skid out of control, possibly flip and roll over. Carol gripped the door as if they were on a roller coaster, which they sort of were. Somehow he understood her greater fear matched his, not for their own safety but for that of all the hapless bystanders. Thankfully they were leaving the city. The streets were starting to empty and flatten. And while that was good news for others, it was bad news for them because it meant visibility was clear with nothing between them and their pursuers who were once again behind them and gaining.

"Carol, take the wheel. I'm going to need to do some fancy shooting."

"Can shooting be fancy?" she muttered, but it was more a question to herself as she slid beneath him and he overtop her, momentarily mashing her into the seat when the wheel jerked as their feet traded places. Jones rolled down the passenger window, stuck the upper half of his body out, and took aim.

The first shot went wide, but the second hit the intended target, blowing out the windshield. It was possible he hit someone in the car, not the driver because it was too far to the side. Even so, the car careened and slowed.

The problem, Jones now realized, was that their car was also slowing.

"What are you doing?" he yelled, shooting Carol a frantic glance.

"I didn't want you to fall out," Carol said, darting him a nervous look.

He thumped the dash. "Don't worry about me. Drive, Carol, just drive."

She gripped the wheel and took off, flattening Jones into the seat behind him. He bonked his head, hard, but couldn't complain because he'd asked her to drive like an insane person. Jones directed her on a circuitous route back to the resort. They made the drive in silence, pulling wearily up the resort's long and winding lane. The guards at the gate regarded him with questioning glances. Jones nodded to them. *Mind your business, boys.* They had never seen him leave the resort with a guest before, an occurrence odd enough to invite curiosity and maybe even speculation. Jones was glad he felt the need to keep his business private because what could he possibly say? *I accidentally yanked a tourist into a murderous disaster plot with armed gangsters? Also, I ate squid.* Nope. Bad enough he'd had to fess up to Ridge. No way would he admit his error to his subordinates. Maybe someday it would be a fun anecdote. *If we survive,* he thought, turning to stare out the window with grim determination. They would make it through this. Somehow now, for better or worse, Carol was his responsibility. Certainly death couldn't be worse than that. Could it?

Carol parked in his assigned slot and turned off the Jeep. "Zero stars, David, would not recommend," she said.

Jones closed his eyes and took a breath. It was going to be a long couple of days.

CHAPTER 15

The walk to Carol's room felt like it took fifteen years, possibly because no less than twelve people stopped Jones to talk.

"It feels like when I was little and used to go to church with my Grandma," Carol noted. "I had a hard time getting her out of there, too."

"I'm a people person," Jones groused, his words running contrary to his grumpy tone. There was something about Carol, though, something that made every observation feel like an accusation. Even the way she eyed him was like nails on a chalkboard.

"You don't have to walk me up. I'm perfectly capable," she huffed.

"I'm doing it," he huffed in return.

"Fine, we're here," she said, pausing to face him in front of her door.

"Good. Great, have a…" Whatever witty retort he was about to expel died on his lips when he realized her door was partially open. Carol hadn't realized yet and put her hand on it, ready to open it. Maybe Jones caught a sight or sound from inside, or maybe his instincts were so finely honed he sensed that something was about to happen. Whatever the reason, he practically lifted Carol out of the way, ignoring her indignant squeak of protest, then used his foot to kick open the door as his hand withdrew his gun. The combination of maneuvers seemed to happen in slow motion but, in reality, probably took all of three seconds, three seconds in which whoever was waiting inside dove for him, tackling him to the ground. Carol squeaked again, jumping aside as their two rolling bodies nearly jostled into her.

The man was part of a gang. Jones could tell by how bulky and strong he was. All of the hapless locals who occasionally got caught breaking into the resort looked as hungry and underfed as they were. Only the illegally funded gangs could afford to eat well enough to develop the kind of muscles Jones was now dealing with.

Though the man was ripped, he wasn't as well trained as Jones. It only took a few defensive maneuvers to buck him off. By the time Jones aimed his gun, the man was squeezing out the window, not bothering to toss Jones or Carol a look before he disappeared.

Jones inspected the luxurious room, making sure no one else was left behind. "Did he take anything?" Jones asked, holstering his gun as he finally turned to face Carol.

She was pressed against the door, gripping the frame with both hands behind her, eyes wide and welded on his. "Carol," he said, voice a little firmer as he tried to snap her back to reality.

She jumped as if he'd slapped her. "Oh," she yelped and scurried toward the closet in a panic. Jones watched while she flung it open and began to rifle her bag.

"What are you looking for?" he asked. What could she have of value in there? Had the gangster actually been sent to retrieve something instead of intimidate or harm her?

"Where is it, where is it," she muttered to herself before holding something aloft and then hugging it to her chest in triumph.

"What is it?" Jones asked, edging closer as his ever-present nosiness got the better of him. He loved being in the know, loved gossip more than most people he knew.

Carol faced him with a beaming smile, revealing what she held near and dear.

He blinked at it and focused on her. "Coffee?"

"Really expensive coffee I bought for my dad," she said with instant indignation at his judgmental tone.

"Did you check your electronics or jewelry?" he asked, resisting the urge to pinch the bridge of his nose. The woman was not normal.

She used the heel of her hand to smack herself upside the forehead. "Oh, no, my diamond tiara. What if he's taken it?" Her eyes rolled as if on a little round track. "I judge rich hotels for a living. If I had anything of actual value, I *still* couldn't afford what this place costs a night." She gave the coffee one more hug, a little sniff, and tucked it back in her case with a pat. "So that's that. I'm glad it's over."

"It's not over," Jones said.

Carol made a show of looking around. "Are you planning to call him back for an exhibition rematch?"

This time he did pinch the bridge of his nose. "He could come back at any time, Carol. If he got in once, he can get in again."

"Um, not to be harsh, but aren't you sort of the head of security here? It seems like there should be something you could do to prevent murderers from breaking in."

"I'm not omnipresent, and there are a lot of people working here who are willing to take an extra payoff to sneak someone in. Or they're being threatened. The point is the resort is too big for me to control exactly who comes in and out or when."

"What can you control?" she asked, crossing her arms in what he already recognized as her Challenge Pose. He was about to get an earful when she stood like that.

"I can control my living quarters," he said.

She remained staring at him, sifting the words, uncomprehending. "Okay, good for you, I guess? But I don't see how that helps me."

"I can keep an eye on you there," he added.

"And then what? I hang out at your place for a few hours and then come back here so he can kill me in my sleep?"

"No, you're going to stay at my place until this is resolved."

Her too-expressive eyes rounded. "Uh, no I'm not. I already told you I have a boyfriend."

"Do you honestly think I'm hitting on you right now? That this is how low I have to sink to get a woman?"

She opened her mouth to answer. He held up his hand like a stop sign to preempt her. "Stop. Don't. Let me try this another way: get your stuff, you're staying with me. In my second bedroom."

"You could have led with that," she grumbled, turning to gather her bag. Jones watched her with barely disguised annoyance, the pad of his thumb pressed hard between his eyes. Inviting her into his inner sanctum felt like losing somehow. Maybe because for the last few months of his employment he had managed to keep it separate, his own space. And now with Carol there it wouldn't be his anymore, would no longer be his Fortress of Solitude.

She shouldered her lone bag and stood surveying the room as if bidding it goodbye. He tried to see it from her point of view. The room was luxurious, but his bungalow wasn't exactly a slum.

"It's not so bad at my place," he said, a peace offering.

"I'm sure it's not, it's just..." She sighed and waved to the room. "Goodbye, Fortress of Solitude."

Biting his cheek to hide his smile, Jones turned and led the way to the hallway.

CHAPTER 16

As he had done when leaving her room, he tried to view his space anew through her eyes. Everything had come standard with his employment, the rattan furniture, the beachy, tropical décor. All Jones added was a bevy of pictures of family and friends. Carol eyed those but didn't go forward to inspect them. Jones let out the breath he'd been holding, relieved. If she had to be in his space, he didn't want her to nosily inspect his things. Or try to horn in and take over, as women were prone to do. It was sparse and Spartan and simple, exactly as he liked it.

"Tidy," Carol noted with approval.

"Navy," he returned, tipping his head to her. "Would you like something to drink?"

"I'd love a cup of tea," she said, perking a little.

He blinked at her. "You realize I'm a guy, right? There's no tea, no potpourri or antimacassars. And the toilet seat stays permanently upright."

"Spoiler alert: it's impossible to assert your maleness in the same sentence you use 'antimacassar,' a word no one has used out of respect for Queen Victoria since her death."

"Admit it, you're just shocked a boiling cauldron of testosterone like me knows and uses big words," he said and, oh, no, did he toss her a flirtatious wink?

"You caught me," she said, but her tone was dry, and he thought he caught the hint of a blush as she turned away from him. "Good thing for you I always carry my own tea. Would his masculineness care for a cup?"

He scratched the side of his nose and tried to look uninterested, even though a hot cup of tea sounded delightful. "It's not, like, girly and fruity, is it?"

She opened her bug-out bag and rifled through. "I usually only carry peach and chamomile, but let me see if I have a spare bag of 'sweaty workout socks' available for you."

"It's lucky for you I consider peach the manliest fruit," he said, sniffing and flexing.

She laughed, an unguarded sound that made him smile. He followed her to the kitchen and perched on a high stool as she made their tea, not bothering to nudge her in the right direction as she rooted in his cupboards for supplies.

She set the water to boil and spent some time staring in his cutlery drawer.

"If you're waiting for it to attack, I have to tell you they're trained to leap only on my command," Jones said.

"Sorry," she said, closing the drawer. "I ponder knives. Occupational hazard."

"Same," Jones said, and he wasn't kidding. He had quite the knife collection. Of a different variety, of course. His could be used for cutting knots or humans, while hers were apparently for cutting chicken and fruit.

"The navy must have been interesting," Carol said, leaning against the counter opposite him.

"That's one word for it," Jones said, recalling with fond nostalgia what had once felt almost insurmountably stressful—the training, the sleeplessness, the travel, the impossible assignments.

"What's the most interesting place you ever traveled?" she asked.

"Some remote parts of Africa. It's like the new frontier of criminal activity. All the world takes advantage of the fact that no one pays attention to what's happening in Africa. Lots of illegal trade: weapons, secrets, drugs, humans."

"What's the most memorable thing you ate while you were there?" she asked, clasping her hands together as her interest piqued. He found it noteworthy that she glossed over all the crime and went straight to food.

"MRE rations," he said.

"David," she exclaimed, jaw dropping as if personally affronted.

He put his hands up, in defense or surrender, he wasn't certain. "I may not be an adventure eater, but I also never spent a few hours rolled into the fetal position, wishing for death after I consumed some food I can't pronounce."

The whistling teapot saved him from her wrathful answer, but not her vengeful glare. She poured their tea and set his in front of him with a sigh and, "You."

He ignored her and sniffed the tea. The scent of peach reminded him of home and he fought a knee-buckling wave of longing.

"Why'd you take this job?" she asked after a minute of surprisingly comfortable silence. "Clearly it wasn't for the travel or the food."

"Money. Most of my friends continued in civil service in some capacity, but it never felt like the right fit for me." Being in the military was one thing, but continuing the life-or-death spy game in real life was another. "Being head of security at a private luxury resort. Who could say no to that?"

"Were your friends jealous of the cushy new position?"

He barked a harsh laugh, remembering the razzing the guys gave him—and still gave—over his new job. "My friends aren't exactly the sort of guys who seek cushiness, comfort, or luxury."

"What do they seek?" she asked.

"Danger, adventure, justice," he supplied.

"But that's not you?" she asked.

"No, it is. Just…"

"What?" she prompted when he paused.

"I guess I was more tuned in to what came after. Some of the guys have families, some are unattached. The ones who have families have either moved away from the crazy danger or made peace with the possibility of not seeing their kids into adulthood. I didn't want to have that worry constantly hanging over me. Someday I want to have a family, and I want to be there for them. Not partially, but fully. Working this job a few years will allow me to retire early, to be fully immersed and present when I'm ready to settle down."

Carol made no reply but her eyes remained securely on his while she sipped her tea. He felt as if she were taking his measure, trying to decide if she could trust him, if she liked him. Strangely he hoped the answer to both those questions was yes. In some odd way she felt like a connection to home. It was more than the fact that she was American. He saw other Americans all the time. It was that sameness he'd felt earlier or, as she'd described, the fact that she was in his lane.

"What about you? Why'd you get into this line of work?"

Her eyes dropped to her cup. "I already told you. I wasn't as good at being a chef as I'd hoped, and I wanted to travel."

"Mm-hmm. And what's the real reason?" he prompted, waiting her out when she squirmed and darted a longing gaze toward her bedroom and escape. At last she took a breath, held it a few beats, and let it out in a rush.

"When I was nine, my little sister got sick. Really sick, like can't-leave-the-house sick. My dad, a welder by day, would come home at night and tell her stories. I'd creep into her room and crawl into her bed and listen while he talked. As he talked, he painted pictures on her walls. He was a good amateur artist, good enough to draw trees and animals and clouds and castles. After a while, every space in her room was filled with his pictures."

"How's your sister now?" he asked, and a part of him didn't want to know because he sensed what the answer would be before she spoke it.

She smiled sadly. "Whole and healed, but no longer here. She didn't make it to her seventh birthday."

"I'm sorry." They observed a minute of solemn silence, taking a few sips of their tea. Again the silence was comfortable, even after the stark revelation. "Is that why you do it?" he said at last. "To live the adventures she never got to?"

"That's what I tell myself," she said.

"What's the real reason?"

"After my sister died, my parents' marriage fell apart. My dad withdrew completely until he eventually stopped calling. He remarried, had more kids. I get a text from him about once a year and a card on Christmas, sent by his wife. I guess," she paused and set down her mug when her hands shook. "I guess what I'm really hoping for is that someday I'll feel worthy of all the pictures on the wall, the ones that weren't for me." She let out a shaky little laugh and fluffed her hair. "Wow, that got deep fast. Sorry for unloading my psychological trauma on you."

"Well, I mean, I did ask," he said, offering her a tentative smile she halfheartedly returned. Now he glimpsed the sameness between them. She had felt left out and excluded by her family; he had felt it from other children. He tipped his mug to her. "To belonging."

She tipped hers to him and they drained the dregs, setting their mugs on the counter at the same time as if they were doing shots at the bar.

"I'll clean these up. You must be exhausted," Jones offered when her gaze darted longingly once more toward her bedroom. Maybe she was tired, or maybe the emotional reveal had been too much for her. Maybe she wanted to retreat and ponder, the same way Jones wanted to.

"Thanks," she said, giving him a little smile that tugged at his heart for its shyness and sincerity. *Sweetie,* he thought as he watched her walk away. *The name's beginning to fit.*

CHAPTER 17

Jones had a hard time falling asleep. Every time he closed his eyes, he pictured little Carol lying in her sister's bed, the combined weight of grief and family exclusion bowing her little shoulders. Tender hearted as he was, he felt her pain, even though it had happened so many years ago. Reaching for the remote on his nightstand, he pushed a button, playing his go-to comfort music. His eyes finally drifted closed when he heard a muffled female voice float through the wall.

"David."

His eyes flapped open. "Yes, Carol."

"Are you listening to Celine Dion?"

He hit the button on his remote so he could be truthful when he answered, "Absolutely no."

There was an echoing silence, and then the sound of muffled laughter, hearty and deep, with a snort thrown in for good measure.

"Carol," he said.

"Yes," she said, hiccupping to get her giggles under control.

"Shaddup."

Her laughter started again, and this time when Jones fell asleep, he was smiling.

*T*he next morning he woke with the barrel of a gun pressed to his forehead.

"I could have killed you four times by now. You're slipping, Jonesie."

"Geroff," Jones mumbled, giving him a shove. "Why you?"

"Cause I'm the best," Ribs said, tucking the gun back into his pack. On closer inspection it was not a gun, but rather a mini flashlight.

Jones made a disgusted little grunt. It wasn't true Ribs was the best, mostly because they were all that good. And they all had their own specialties. Before he could respond further, Ribs took a leap, landing hard on the bed beside him. Jones eyed him with horror.

"Dude, no. What is happening? This isn't a sleepover. Get out of my bed. So many levels of guy code broken at this moment."

"Eh, twenty hour flight," Ribs groaned, rubbing his eyes. Jones knew the feeling well, a combination of exhaustion and desiccation, as if the airline had found a way to secretly suck all moisture from your body as the flight progressed. "Give me the rundown here. What's up?"

"What did Ridge tell you?" Jones asked.

"That you got in a spot of trouble and needed a hand."

Jones let out a relieved breath.

"And that a woman is involved." Ribs tossed him a grin. "Is she hot? I bet she's hot. You got all befuddled and mangled it. Don't worry, Jonesie, your wingman is here. Unless she's uber hot, then dibs."

Jones groaned and rubbed his own eyes. Next door, the shower started.

"Ah, man, I should have peeked in while she was sleeping," Ribs lamented.

"She's not hot," Jones snapped. He realized that, as usual and like the rest of their team, Ribs was merely trying to get to him. Why it was working was a bigger mystery. By now Jones had become impervious to their teasing. Maybe it was being away from them for so long. Maybe he'd lost teasing immunity.

Ribs's face pulled into a grimace. "She's an uggo? Janky teeth? Stank breath? Lumpy bod?"

"Why are you talking like we're in the middle of filming a rap video where they're dubbing all the filthy words for outdated clean ones?" Jones asked.

Ribs snorted and nudged him with an elbow. "Come on, what's up? I need fair warning if I have to try and control my reaction to her hideousness. How's this?" He pressed his lips together and tipped his head, mimicking a grave reserve that could not be faker.

"She's not ugly. She's cute. But she's...she's so..." He broke off, trying to find a proper descriptor for Carol's aggravating nature. "She's the type of person who has to grow on you."

"What's that mean?" Ribs asked. "She crazy? Cause you know I like crazy."

"She's...she's so... She's so *Carol*," he finished, sighing.

"Carol? Like Christmas Carol?" Ribs said.

"As if she's never heard that one before," Jones said, jostling him. "Grow up."

Next door the shower finished. They listened as the hair dryer began and then, a while later, the door wrenched open.

"She's fast," Ribs said.

"She's low maintenance on the looks front," Jones said. Carol was a no-nonsense person. Her hair was an easy style and if she wore makeup, he couldn't tell. So far the most he'd seen her do was apply copious amounts of lip balm and sunscreen.

"Ugly," Ribs said, nodding knowledgably.

"She's not," Jones said, with no idea why he suddenly felt so defensive on Carol's behalf. A day ago he couldn't stand her. Now he felt... protective. But maybe that was it; he'd brought this calamity upon her and it was now his job to see her through.

"Let's go see," Ribs said in a tone that meant he was up to no good. In other words, his usual tone. Jones wanted to caution him one more time to tread carefully, to give her space. But he wasn't sure how he'd take it. Sometimes Ribs did the opposite of what he was told, "sometimes" meaning when he was awake.

They stepped into the kitchen together. Carol whirled to face them, eyebrows shooting high on first sight of Ribs. Jones couldn't tell what Ribs's face looked like and didn't want to know. The odd protective feeling toward Carol had intensified. He didn't want to have to be mad at his friend on her behalf.

"Carol, this is Ribs. He was sent to help us. Ribs, Carol." Jones waved halfheartedly between them. He was certain his manners were lacking in the introduction, but he was also certain he didn't care.

"Oh," Carol said, eyes as bright and sharp as her tone. Jones cringed inwardly, waiting for her to put Ribs on blast in some way. Then about swallowed his tongue when she stepped forward and hugged him. Tightly. Ribs looked questioningly down at Jones over the top of her head. There was no question of returning her hug because she had his arms pinned to his sides. Jones shrugged, torn between befuddlement and resentment. Carol didn't seem like the hugging type. Also, why did Ribs get hugs and he hadn't?

"Thank you," Carol said, giving him one more squeeze before letting go and stepping back. She beamed up at him. "You must have had a long, exhausting flight. Are you hungry?"

"Famished," Ribs said, returning her grin.

"I'm hungry, too," Jones inserted pitifully.

"Of course you are," Carol said, waving her hand at him without turning to look. Her offhand, dismissive manner told him he mattered to her as much as an interfering gnat. "Are eggs okay?"

"Perfect," Ribs answered because, once again, the conversation had been directed to him.

"Eggs are fine for me, too," Jones added pointedly. Carol finally looked at him, cute little nose wrinkled. But it was Ribs who spoke.

"Simmer down, Jonesie. What's got your hackles up?"

"He's always like this," Carol noted, as if Jones wasn't standing right there between them like an interfering toddler.

"Jonesie? No way," Ribs said. "He's the sweetest guy I know."

"David? No way," Carol said, turning her speculative gaze on him. "Hmm, you couldn't tell it by me."

"Hadn't you better get to work on breakfast, *Sweetie*?" he said and waited for the snap back. Then Ribs would know what he'd been dealing with, exactly why he was so short-tempered and out of patience. The woman was a menace. But, like the menace she was, she smiled sweetly and agreed.

"And so I should. You two sit tight. This will only take a minute." She whirled toward the refrigerator and began pulling out ingredients. Meanwhile Ribs thumped Jones in the chest. Hard.

What's wrong with you? he mouthed.

Me? It's not me. It's her. She is making me crazy. You have no idea. She's the human equivalent of having a toothpick jammed in your eyeball, Jones mouthed in return.

Ribs blinked at him. *What?*

So maybe he should have stuck with a shoulder shrug instead of a rant-laced, mouthed paragraph. He shrugged now and they sat.

"Anything we can do?" Ribs asked, as if he'd ever set foot in a kitchen before or had any idea of what to do in one. Ribs's idea of gourmet was eating inside McDonald's instead of getting takeout.

"No, I'm fine, thank you. I could do this in my sleep," Carol said. The two men watched her pivot gracefully around the small kitchen, making whatever she was doing look as effortless and easy as breathing. Deftly, she cracked eggs into a bowl and added salt.

"Are you making omelets?" Jones asked, his mouth already watering.

"Yes, I am," Carol said.

"I'm out of cheese," he noted.

"Omelets don't have cheese in them," she said.

"Of course they do. I've never had an omelet without cheese," he said.

"Then you've never had an omelet," she countered.

Ribs snickered.

Jones pinched his nose. "Omelets have cheese, Carol. It's sort of the universally accepted mode of omelet production that they have cheese."

"No, it's the *American* idea of omelets. French omelets do not have cheese."

"You hate America," Jones accused.

"I love America, but I also know there's more to life than processed food," Carol said.

"I don't like omelets without cheese," Jones said. Even to his own ears he sounded pouty and petulant.

"Then I guess you won't be eating," Carol said in the stern tone that set his teeth on edge. She resumed her task and Jones gave Ribs a pointed look. *You see what I'm dealing with here.*

Ribs shook his head at him. *What is wrong with you?*

A few minutes later he forgot his annoyance. Coincidentally it was the same moment Carol set a fluffy, buttery yellow, perfectly rolled omelet in front of him, with a side of perfectly cubed little squares of fruit.

CHAPTER 18

"Why do they call you Ribs?"

Jones made a mewling little sound that might have been a whimper. They both darted him a questioning glance, but he was too enraptured to feel embarrassment over the sound. Or maybe he was too busy devouring his omelet. Who knew eggs and salt and butter could taste so good? And the fruit…

"Where did this come from?" Jones asked, holding a little cube of something pink aloft on his fork. He knew for certain he had no fruit in his bungalow.

"From my purse," Carol said offhandedly, her attention already back on Ribs and waiting for his answer.

"You carry purse fruit?" Jones asked.

"You don't?" she said, flicking her fingers in annoyance at him, presumably for interrupting, although it could be for anything. Apparently he rubbed her wrong the way she rubbed him wrong; in all the ways.

Ribs snickered and dabbed his mouth with his napkin like a debutante before answering. "All the guys get a handle."

If she was daunted by the way he glided around her question, she didn't show it. "But why Ribs? What's it for?" She tipped her head and eyed him. "Did you used to be super skinny?"

Ribs darted a glance to Jones, either asking permission or advice. Their handles were private, something kept between their team. Only a select few got to learn why they existed. Jones gave a little nod and Ribs lifted his shirt. Carol gasped, eyeing him, her mouth ajar.

"Wow." She cleared her throat. "I get it now. It's because your abs are so defined they look like actual ribs."

Ribs laughed, a loud guffaw of delight.

Jones ducked around him, inspecting his abs. "What? No, that's not… We all have abs like that, okay? It's because of this." He grabbed Ribs's arm and used it to angle him to the side. This time Carol gasped with the appropriate amount of horror.

"Is that…" she began.

"Shark bite," Ribs said, his fingers unconsciously finding the groove of each wedge-shaped scar. And then everybody went silent. Carol was likely asking herself how he could possibly still be alive with a bite that large. Jones was asking himself the same question. He remembered the exact moment it happened, Ridge's second month as their team leader. They had a black op assignment in a hostile country, so hostile they had to be dropped into the ocean at night and swim to shore. For a group of SEALs, a night swim was a piece of cake. But no one warned them the waters were so shark-infested.

"My suit took the brunt of it," Ribs said, pulling his shirt down and giving it a self-conscious tug. It probably wasn't the scar that bothered him, so much as the fear he'd felt that night, the fear they'd all felt. Jones could still hear his scream in his head, could remember the horrible sight of Ribs being yanked under the water for that brief second. He punched the shark, hard, and the shark learned quickly the strange morsel was not a helpless seal. It swam away, but there were a dozen others and the bloody holes in Ribs acted as a beacon to them all.

They'd grabbed him and hightailed it to shore, taking turns swimming him in while the others surrounded him in a formation and kept the sharks at bay. When they finally made it to shore, Ridge had been the one to rip off his suit and triage the damage, patching Ribs with the emergency kit, shooting him with morphine. And then they'd stashed him and completed their mission, leaving Shimmer to babysit until they returned.

That had been the easy part. Getting out of hostile territory with a shark bit brother had been the harrowing part. But it had solidified their team, along with their trust in their new leader. That, like so many other things, had bonded them for life, all of them.

Carol reached forward and gave Ribs's wrist a comforting squeeze. "I'm so sorry. That must have been awful." And then she surprised Jones by squeezing his wrist, too, making him wonder what his expression looked like. Was it any wonder so many former soldiers went crazy? Who could possibly understand the weight of the secrets they had to carry? Besides other soldiers, of course.

"Chicks dig it," Ribs said, tossing her a wink that made her smile. Or maybe it was his newly buoyant tone. And, knowing Ribs, it was probably true. He radiated a danger signal women seemed to enjoy. Unlike Jones. Somehow no matter what he did, women seemed to find him soft and cozy and so unbearably *safe.*

"Do you have a girl?" Carol asked, resting her chin in her hand as she regarded Ribs.

"He has several," Jones inserted.

"Don't be snide, David. You and Ribs are clearly different types," Carol said.

I love her, Ribs mouthed as soon as Carol turned toward the sink to grab a refill of coffee.

No, Jones mouthed in reply.

Ribs pointed to Jones and then to Carol.

NO, Jones mouthed again, waving his hands to ward away the suggestion.

"Mosquitoes?" Carol guessed, facing them again.

"No, something much more annoying and insidious," Jones said. Ribs snorted. Smiling benignly, Carol topped off his coffee. Jones held out his mug. She ignored him and returned the pot to the burner.

"What?" she asked, finally noting his indignation.

"You are…that is…I can't with the…" Jones floundered, unable to find words for how badly she aggravated him.

Carol eyed Ribs. "How did you guys handle his unending crankiness?"

"We never had to," Ribs said, studying Jones, his head tilted like a curious kitten. "I've never seen him grumpy before. Didn't actually know he had it in him. Huh."

Jones pinched the bridge of his nose. Ribs was making assertions, Jones could tell. And he shouldn't be, not about this situation, not about anything. If Jones *was* cranky, which he definitely wasn't, then it was certainly justified by Carol's incessantly annoying behavior. The woman was certifiable and apparently it was contagious because he felt like he was slowly losing his mind, especially when Ribs looked at him like he was the crazy one. He tried once again to explain. "You don't…she is…I'm not…"

"Do you know they have corporate communication seminars that could help you learn how to talk better? Might take you farther up the ladder," Carol suggested and Ribs sputtered a laugh he tried to turn into a cough.

Jones couldn't reply because he was breathing too hard, puffing little bursts of oxygen like a perturbed bull. His hands itched, to do what he had no idea. It's not like he could choke the woman with Ribs sitting there, he would definitely frown on that sort of thing. And it wasn't as if Jones was given to unprovoked violence of any kind, especially against a woman. But Carol was testing his limits in all the ways.

Unaware of how close she was to being throttled, she smiled brightly. "Can you excuse me a moment? I need to send a text." Still beaming, she gave a friendly little pat to Ribs's shoulder and breezed from the room.

CHAPTER 19

Carol knew the exact moment she was in trouble. When the swarthy man lifted his shirt and she saw his abs, abs that looked like they'd been precision cut with a laser on a production line, she gave them a glance and focused on David instead. David, who looked like he'd been formed on that same production line, only in Play-Doh, so it made him squishy and touchable, as if someone drew him with a pencil and then smudged all the edges, softening them. And so it was that the second man she was attracted to in her entire life was a security guard, thousands of miles from anything and anyone familiar. Not her style, not her style at all.

She withdrew her phone and sent an SOS text. *Halp!*

What?? Why did you spell like that? The return text came immediately, despite the late hour where the recipient lived.

So you would know it was a figurative emergency and not literal, Carol replied.

What is figurative emergency?

Carol frowned at her phone. *Did someone rob you and steal all your extra words? Why are you typing like you're writing fortune cookies?*

Nursing baby using me as chew. Typing one hand, came the reply.

Carol smiled, imagining the cozy picture. In culinary school she'd been roommates with three other women. They'd bonded in the way only poverty, youth, and enthusiasm can bind people, meaning they were lifers, despite the fact that she hadn't seen some of them since graduation. The particular friend she now texted, Poppy Dunbar, rather Poppy Dunbar Langford, thanks to her hasty elopement, was as close to her as anyone on earth, and yet she hadn't seen her in person in five long years. *I need baby snuggles,* Carol replied.

Visit, Poppy replied.

Carol sighed. She would love to visit, especially right now in her current debacle. She would guess there was nowhere farther on earth from David Jones than Poppy's tiny town in West Texas. Even he, with all his fancy Navy SEAL assignments, had probably never heard of her friend's new tiny hometown. *Maybe someday.*

In return, Poppy sent her a rolling eye emoji, most likely because she knew it wasn't true. Carol traveled the entire year. And for those few days when she wasn't traveling she was in Maine with Brody and Georgette, Brody's sister. Which brought her full circle to the reason she was texting Poppy in the first place. *There's this guy.*

Uh...Brody?

Poppy knew Brody, of course. Georgette was one of their fearsome foursome, along with Sparrow, wild child and current bad girl of the chef world. Brody had been a near permanent fixture at their tiny New York apartment. He had taken the role of protective big brother to new heights, personally screening all of Georgette's roommates before she was allowed to live with them. That was the first day Carol met him, as a bright-eyed eighteen year old, on her own and in search of a roommate. She had fallen hard for his strong silent type vibes and, she wasn't going to lie, ridiculous good looks. The feeling hadn't been mutual. Carol had never tricked herself into believing she was the bombshell sort who made men drool. Slow and steady wins the race could be her life motto. Eventually, a year after culinary school, Brody began showing interest. From there they fell seamlessly into a pleasant and easy relationship, one where they spent exactly five days a year together, texting and trading photos the other three hundred sixty. *Is that enough for me?* It was the first time Carol had ever asked herself the question. For so long Brody had been her ideal. He was solid, dependable, kind, and good. But he didn't share her love of adventure. Or travel. Or food. She thought of him like her anchor, tethering her to her home country, holding a place for her while she worked through her boundless wanderlust. But what if it was more than that? What if they were each other's security blankets? What if they were holding on to each other so they didn't have to do the hard work of finding someone else, didn't have to face the possible rejection of meeting someone new?

Not Brody.

Uh-oh. Spill.

I met a boy on vacation.

RUN AWAY. VACATION BOYS ARE NEVER THE RIGHT ONES.

Ummm, didn't you marry a boy you met on vacation? Carol reminded her. Poppy had a fling with her Sully that turned into a baby, that then turned into marriage, that then turned into love. Carol hadn't been able to attend the wedding or reception, but she'd seen multiple pictures and, yowza, she totally got it. Only someone who looked and acted like Texas Ranger Sully Langford could settle her free-spirited, driven little Poppy.

Yes, but...shaddup. You know the stats. USUALLY it doesn't work out. I'm the exception, obvi. Plus we're different. You're Carol. You're RELIABLE.

YOU TAKE THAT BACK, POPPY LANGFORD, Carol typed. Reliable. Ugh. She was *not* reliable. She was a world traveler. She'd been more places the last year than most people visited in a lifetime.

Stop shouting, Grandma. That's why we love you. So the sun rises and sets, our Carol will always be our Carol. You may love adventure travel, but deep down you're steady. Calm waters. You're our Sweetie!

This boy thinks I'm awful, Carol informed her.

HAHAHAHAHAHA. No he doesn't because it's not possible. You're best person I know, best person anyone knows.

Carol could only imagine David's reaction if she showed him Poppy's text. He wouldn't believe it. He would bluster and stammer and point at her, adorable cheeks flushing with anger. *I'm seriously screwing everything up here, Poppy. HALP.*

Take a deep breath. Rewind. Forget other boy, no matter how cute. Focus on you. Is Brody what you want? If so, run away from cute boy. If not, cut the tether.

YOU'RE SUPPOSED TO TELL ME EXACTLY WHAT TO DO, NOT GIVE WISE ADVICE TO MAKE ME FIGURE IT OUT FOR MYSELF. MOTHERHOOD AND MARRIAGE HAVE RUINED YOU. GIVE ME BACK MY WILD, THOUGHTLESS POPPY!!

Grown up now. Deal. Also stop screaming. Giving me virtual headache. Also going to need secret photo of boy so I can judge him by his hotness. If too hot, then merely temp insanity and vacation overload. Worth a fling, not worth getting flung.

FORTUNE COOKIE SAYS WHAT?? Carol replied.

Shut it. Am wise and junk. Wiser while being chewed on by baby in middle of night. By the time baby gets all teeth, will be renowned philosopher.

Carol smiled, stroking a finger affectionately over her phone. *Thanks. I love you much.*

Love you, too.

Carol paused and typed the part she was reluctant to send. *Will you still love me if I break up with Brody?*

ABSOLUTELY!

Will Georgette still love me? Carol tried.

The little text bubble hovered for a long time before Poppy eventually replied. *I think yes. You know GG, she feels things deep. But eventually we'll all move on and deal. Do what's best for you. Baby is finally asleep. Fortune Cookie out.*

When Carol returned to the kitchen, she inadvertently interrupted what looked like a heated debate between Jones and Ribs.

"Let it go," Jones hissed before realizing Carol was once again in the room. He tried and failed to muster a smile and she tried and failed not to be hurt by that.

"Sorry to interrupt," she said.

"It's fine," Jones said.

"We were talking about you," Ribs said at the same moment. Jones made a hissing sound like a radiator emptying itself of steam. "Jonesie was bringing me up to date on the case and all the trouble you're in. I think there's only one obvious solution."

"Send her home," Jones said.

"Use her as bait," Ribs said at the same time. Jones hissed again, longer and more expressively this time.

"You can't. She's a civilian. Besides, she would hate it," Jones said.

"I would love it," Carol said, clapping her hands excitedly.

"Good, it's settled," Ribs said.

"It's not settled," Jones argued. "Look at her." Her motioned toward Carol who, nervous at being cast into the center of attention, gave an awkward parade float wave. "She's not a spook. She's a..." he snapped his fingers at Carol, urging her to fill in the blank.

"Classically trained chef," Carol supplied.

"Right. A classically trained chef. And a..." Jones prompted.

"Corporate spy," Carol added helpfully.

"Corporate spy. *Corporate.* What does she know about actual spying?"

"Probably a lot," Ribs said. "She knows how to be sneaky, how to keep a cover. She doesn't have to do any of the heavy lifting or danger work because we'll do that."

"But *look at her*," Jones said. Carol waved again. He huffed and settled his arm on her shoulders, facing her toward Ribs. "She's little and guileless and cute. She has a dimple, for goodness sake."

"I have two, actually," Carol inserted, pulling her cheek up hard to make her second dimple pop.

"Two dimples." Jones tossed the declaration toward Ribs like an indictment.

"So do you, Jonesie," Ribs reminded him.

"That's different. I've had the training. I was a SEAL."

"Carol was in the CIA," Ribs said, high fiving her.

"That's not...you can't...she wasn't..."

"Uh-oh, you broke him again," Carol said.

Jones swiped his free hand over his face. His other arm was still around Carol's shoulders, unconsciously aligning them together against Ribs. What he didn't understand was how everything in his world had gone wrong since he met her. How had it gotten so mixed up, so upside down? She was a train wreck of epic proportions, yet everyone called her Sweetie. Even Ribs, who was usually cynical about women, had somehow been duped into believing Carol was normal. But she wasn't. She *wasn't*. Jones could see the truth, even if no one else could. And he had to protect her, even if no one else would. She might get on his ever loving last nerve, but he didn't want anything to happen to her.

"Jones, it's going to be okay," Ribs said.

"How can you possibly say that?" Jones asked.

"Because we have these on our side," Ribs said, lifting his shirt to display his magnificent abs again. And Carol clapped for him, feeding his already too-big ego.

"You look like you should be on a recruitment poster somewhere," she told him.

"Don't say things like that to him. He doesn't need to hear them," Jones told her.

"But you look good, too, David. More realistic. Just right, actually," she said and then surprised him by turning slightly to hug his waist in a move that was shockingly reassuring.

"Oh," Jones stammered, cheeks flushing with an embarrassing blush. It wasn't that women didn't find him attractive, but usually it was when he was on his own. It rarely to never happened when he was with one of his Adonis-looking teammates. "Um." He patted her back a couple of times. "Thanks, I guess." He hated that Ribs was bearing witness to this. It would fuel the unending supply of teasing his teammates always had at the ready for him. But when Ribs spoke, he sounded normal. Normal for him, albeit.

"I actually was asked to be on a recruitment poster. Then they saw the teeth marks and said no." He motioned to his massive scar. "I guess they were afraid it would frighten away the newbies."

Carol faced him, frowning. "That's outrageous. They should want to attract the people who aren't afraid of a shark bite."

"To be fair, I don't think there's anyone who isn't afraid of shark bites," Jones inserted, belatedly realizing he and Carol were still canoodling. How? And why? She was like a ghost, sneaking past his defenses in all the ways.

"Do you want me to write a strongly worded letter to them?" Carol offered. "I am amazing at strongly worded letters."

"I'll keep that in mind," Ribs said, ruffling her hair in a way that caused both her cheeks to dimple in response. There was something abnormal here, something greatly amiss. Ribs did not warm up to women easily, and now he and Carol were like long lost brother and sister who had finally been reunited. How was it possible Ribs didn't see how completely annoying and overbearing she was? And, more importantly, WHY WAS HE STILL HUGGING HER? He dropped his arms and took a step back, rifling his hair. Did she perform some kind of voodoo curse on them to make them act this way?

Ribs and Carol regarded him with matching expressions, like he was the one with a problem when clearly it was both of them. "So, to be clear, we are not using Carol as bait. She is not part of this operation. No discussion, the end."

Ribs and Carol continued to stare at him with the same stoic expression. Then they turned to each other and smiled. "Let's plan," Carol said, clapping her hands together.

"Let's," Ribs agreed, mimicking her. They sat down together, leaving Jones hovering at the edge of the room like the outsider he now was.

CHAPTER 20

After their planning session, where Jones hovered at the edge of the room and made disapproving clucking noises like a fussy den mother, Ribs decided to "crash," after his all night flight.

"You didn't used to need a nap after an all nighter, but I understand if you're feeling your age now, sir," Jones told him. The guys might love to razz him about his innocence and big heart, but he could always get them on the age and stamina, especially because Jones was younger than most of them, if only by a couple of years. "Want me to warm you some milk, Grandpa?"

"Nah, just go ahead and enjoy the gift of time I'm giving you," Ribs said, waving his hand like a fairy godfather toward Carol.

"*No*," Jones mouthed, afraid Carol would overhear. He had no idea why Ribs now had it in his head that he and Carol were destined to be together, but somehow he was vaguely insulted by it. Carol was cute, maybe even adorable, but she wasn't one of those women, the kind his teammates always somehow ended up paired with, the kind they playingly fought over the privilege to woo and win. Jones had never been included in that sort of competition, and now he saw why: they didn't see him as capable of winning one of those women. They saw him worthy of women like Carol—cute women, quirky women, *nice* women. Jones was so tired of nice and normal his teeth ached. Just once he wanted to be that guy, the one who got the woman with the heart-stopping good looks with legs for miles, the one all the other guys wanted. And, really, what was wrong with wanting? Nothing, not a thing. He refused to settle for *nice* because it was what everyone expected of him.

Now when he wanted space the most, when he would have been happy for some of the space and alone time he had so recently eschewed, he was stuck with Carol. Ribs abandoned them for sleep, and he couldn't leave her alone, not when her life was in danger because of him. So she tagged along, observing everything he showed her with clinical detachment and PhD-level absorption, taking notes in her little book.

"Carol."

"Yes, David." She glanced up at him from her crouch and he momentarily forgot what he was going to say because, okay, she actually was adorable, with her little turned up freckled nose, dimpled cheeks, and fringed lashes. Like a baby doll you wanted to pick up because it looked so lovable and cozy.

"Is it actually necessary to inspect the laundry chute that closely?" He had taken her on what was supposed to be a quick tour of the resort, one in which he impressed her with the place. Not only had she spent such an inordinate amount of time inspecting each and every atom of space, but she had found fault with all of it, making copious notes in her book of doom.

She straightened and smoothed a hand on her dress, righting it after it stuck to her and made her look like her legs were on sideways. "Yes."

"Why? Why do you have to be so nitpicky?" *Why can't you enjoy life without finding fault in every blessed thing,* was what he wanted to say.

"Because I'm paid to be. Kind of a lot of money, actually."

"How do rusty bolts on a laundry chute help the overall function of this resort?" he demanded.

"Are you familiar with the broken window theory?" she asked.

"Obviously," he said, a blatant lie because he had no idea what she was talking about. But it seemed like he should and he couldn't stand to lose face in front of her. For whatever reason, it felt to him as if they were locked in some kind of strong and silent competition, one he'd been losing since he met her.

She smiled, clearly disbelieving him. "The broken window theory asserts that big problems do not begin as big problems. They begin as little problems. Violent crime in a neighborhood doesn't begin as violent crime. It begins as silent neglect, a little bit of graffiti, a broken window here and there. And if you clean up the little things, the big things will also resolve."

"Okay. Extrapolate that out for me. How does this broken bolt apply to bettering the resort?"

Carol took his finger and ran it gently over the broken bolt. "Do you feel that sharp edge? It grabs onto sheets and towels, ripping them. Two of my sheets and three towels are ripped on the edges, with rust stains." She tapped his finger against the rusty bolt. "Clean laundry at a five star resort is imperative. It's also impossible when it's coming out rusted and frayed. Fix the bolt, fix the laundry."

"Huh," he murmured softly. Not only did he suddenly get her point, but it felt kind of nice, her fingers gently smoothing over his. When was the last time he held hands with a woman? He was sappy enough to admit it was one of his favorite parts, that he enjoyed the build up to a relationship as much as the relationship itself. Not that he'd had so many of those. But there was enough of the insecure former fat kid in him to get a ridiculous little thrill every time he held a woman's hand or leaned in for that first kiss.

His eyes fell on Carol's lips, pursed slightly as she stared at the laundry chute in concentration, her fingers still absently pressing his to the bolt, caressing a little as they made each pass. What would it be like to kiss Carol? He realized the direction of his thoughts and yanked his hand back, wiping it on his pants a few times to try and erase the sensation. If anyone was going to kiss Carol, it would be her serious boyfriend, Maine Cop, another surprise. He imagined her with an accountant or something equally subdued. A cop was unexpected. But to each her own. Maybe she had a thing for guys who lived dangerously. *Guys like me. No, strike that. Also, shut up.*

"Lunch?" he asked, snagging her attention. She turned to him with a cheerful smile.

"What did you have in mind?"

"Noon buffet has hot dogs," he said.

"Do they also have corn and mashed potatoes?" she asked, her enthusiasm matching his.

He nodded.

"No," she said deadpan, enthusiasm disappearing.

"What? Why not?"

"Because corn doesn't grow here. That corn probably came from America."

"What's wrong with America?" he asked, feeling defensive on behalf of the country he'd fought for.

"Absolutely nothing. God bless it. But it's thousands of miles away. Do you know how old that corn is by now? In corn years, it would be toothless and incontinent."

"Corn doesn't have years," he said, pinching the bridge of his nose. "It's corn. Don't anthropomorphize the things I'm about to eat. It's creepy."

She stepped forward and clasped his hand, giving it a little tug. "You are in the middle of some of the best, most amazing fruit and vegetation on the planet, near some truly incredible local cuisine. Take a leap, try something new."

"I don't like new," Jones said.

She took another little step closer, until they were chest to chest, not touching but almost. "You have ideas about things. Doesn't mean they're correct."

Was she still talking about food? Surely she couldn't know what he'd been thinking about her. The proximity and angle of their bodies made it feel natural to reach out and rest his fingers on her hips. "No tofu. I draw the line at soy."

"Don't you trust me?" she asked.

He had no idea what he felt in relation to her. Everything felt muddled and getting murkier by the moment. Why was he touching this strange woman who drove him insane?

"I'm starving," Carol said, words soft and sultry. Was she staring at his lips or was that his imagination? "I really need…" she inched slightly closer.

"Yes?" he croaked.

"Pad Thai," she breathed. "With shrimp curry."

"Noodles? You're thinking of noodles right now?" he asked.

She grasped his shirt in both her hands and gave it a little shake. "Spoiler alert, David: I'm always thinking of noodles. Come on, I'll make a plate for you."

"No tofu, swear it," Jones said, following her as she turned toward the cafeteria.

"No tofu," she agreed.

"And no…" he began, but she put up a hand and cut him off.

"You only get one veto."

"What? Since when?"

"Since I decided you don't know what's good for you and took control of your diet," she said.

"You can't do that," he said.

"I have to."

"Why?"

"Because this is my mission, to proselytize those living in food darkness. You think you're living a full life because you've traveled and you live in this exotic paradise, but really you've continued to live on the farm where you grew up in different places. I only have a few days to open your eyes and help enlighten you."

"I'm not…that's not…" Realizing he was once again sputtering in irritation, he took a deep breath and tried again. "Who says I grew up on a farm?"

"Did you?" she asked.

"Sort of. My grandparents had a farm," he admitted.

"In the middle of the country, I'll bet."

"Nebraska," he said, once again feeling like he'd lost something but not knowing what. Why should it matter if she knew things about him, things he usually kept hidden from others? For some reason he tried to play down his squeaky clean farm boy image. It didn't exactly go well with the lothario image he tried to project to women he found interesting. Instead of, "That's hot," the reaction he usually got was, "That's adorable."

"Lucky," Carol said.

"Why lucky?"

"To have that kind of heritage, that connection to land, to history and culture. It's enviable."

Certainly no one had ever envied his grandparents' tiny farm in their tiny Nebraska town. When he was little, Jones loved the farm. He couldn't wait to go there each summer, loved how his grandparents put him to work and gave him so much responsibility. As he grew into a teenager, he still loved it, but he kept that love hidden because it was mixed with embarrassment. Everyone else had grandparents who looked the same age as his parents, had large houses, an overabundance of money and nice cars. No one had grandparents as plainspoken, hardworking, and impoverished as his. No one else had to spend his summer working from dawn to dusk to help them make ends meet, to help them have enough food and chopped wood for winter. Really, he should thank them. If not for all those days upon days chopping wood when he was a teenager, he might never have lost his extra weight and made it as a SEAL.

"Are you coming with me, or do you want me to surprise you? No, never mind. If you come, you'll get plain noodles. Find a seat, please, and I'll bring our food," Carol directed, walking away without waiting for a reply. Jones stood helplessly in the middle of the cafeteria. His gaze drifted toward the American section of the buffet. Part of him yearned for his daily hot dog. The other part of him couldn't stop envisioning geriatric corn, bent over a walker and dribbling butter. *Blast you, Carol.* If she ruined corn for him, he might never forgive her.

He ambled to a table and waited, cheeks resting in his fists. Carol returned in short order, balancing three loaded plates of food. She sat them on the table and fussed a bit, arranging them between them. Something about the scene was cozy and reminded Jones of the way his mother used to fuss over his food, as if she cared about his well-being and wanted to make certain he enjoyed it.

"What am I eating?" he asked as he picked up a fork and loaded it with long and skinny noodles.

"Tofu," Carol said and rolled her eyes when he froze. "I'm joking. You really lack a sense of humor about soy. It's Pad Thai and a few other things." Her fork clinked against his, urging him to continue. "Fair warning, this is the hot section. I dumped a bunch of garlic chili sauce on everything because it's my favorite. I like the way it makes my lips burn."

"Weird," he murmured, but he also stared at her lips as he chewed, wondering if it would make his lips burn if he kissed her.

"What?" she asked, using her napkin to dab her chin.

"Nothing." He shook his head. They ate a few bites in silence. Like the night before, Jones was shocked by how delicious everything tasted. He felt like his taste buds were exploding, albeit in a good way. Of course he didn't volunteer that information. No need to make her smug. Also like the night before they shared plates. It was strange how comfortably they'd fallen into their new little routine.

"So I notice you didn't go gaga for Ribs," Jones said after a bit of oddly comfortable and companionably silent chewing.

"I take it that's a thing that routinely happens," Carol said.

"Yep," Jones returned.

"I have friends like that. It's the worst. I guess I've never been accused of going with the crowd and being like everybody else. Plus I'm always that woman, friend woman. I automatically assign myself to the Friendzone. Saves time and energy."

"I hear that," Jones said, holding his fork aloft in a little salute. "Lemme see a picture of the boyfriend." What if he wasn't real? What if she was lying? What if she came to the island in order to troll for men? What if *he* was being trolled and he didn't even realize?

She fished for her phone, made a few swipes, and turned it to face him. He wiped his fingers and took the phone, pulling it closer for a look. The first thing he noted was Carol, but a cleaned up version, her hair nicely curled and wearing more makeup with a dress that hugged her curves pleasantly, much more so than the amorphous sun dress she wore today. *Maybe not trolling, then.* If she were trolling, she would definitely reveal those curves instead of cover them as if she were in denial about their existence.

Next his gaze moved to the guy, lingering in surprise. "Looks like he could have been on our team," he noted. He was tall, much taller than Carol, with broad shoulders and an athletic build. Swap his face out and he could have been Ridge or Ethan or Ribs or any of the others.

"I think he had aspirations in that direction, but his parents died in a car accident his senior year of high school. He didn't want to leave his sister, Georgette." She reached for her phone, but Jones held onto it, tipping his head as if making a detailed study of the guy, which he was.

"He doesn't look like he belongs in your lane," Jones said, finally releasing the phone. "He looks like one of them. The others. The sort you accused me of aiming for instead of staying in my lane."

Carol snatched her phone back. "Don't be ridiculous. He's not like that." She turned the phone around, making her own perusal. "The thing about Brody is that... He's, well, you have to understand that..." She paused and frowned at the phone a few beats before setting it aside and bursting into noisy tears.

"Oh. Uh-oh. Oh, no," Jones fussed, feeling helpless. He hated seeing a woman cry. He was used to seeing his teammates bring women to tears. It had never been him before. "Don't cry," he said, reaching across the table to poke her bicep.

"You are so bad at this," Carol said, grabbing a wad of napkins. She pressed them to her eyes, either trying to absorb or stop the flow of water.

"I'm actually not," Jones said. With a sigh he scooted closer and put his arms around her, pulling her against him. He'd been right to resist the action because it felt a bit too right, like the final piece of a puzzle clicking into place. He wondered if Carol felt it too because she nuzzled, fitting her face nicely in the niche between his chin and shoulder.

"I didn't mean it as an insult," he soothed, running his hand gently over her head. Then he used that hand to wave to a passerby who tossed him a dirty look, somehow sensing he was the cause of Carol's tears.

"I know. I wasn't insulted. It's not you. It's Brody."

His arms tightened. "What about him?" Was he abusive? A deadbeat? Lowlife? Loser?

"He's so good, so completely perfect," Carol wailed.

Oh. "Sorry?" he tried.

"Haven't you ever wanted something so badly, been so certain it was the right thing? And then you got it and it didn't match the picture in your head?"

"Incessantly. All the time," Jones said, and he meant it. Every woman he'd ever dated, even this job couldn't live up to the impossible standard in his head.

"How do you fix it?" she asked.

"You either let go of the picture in your head or…"

"Or?" she prompted when he didn't continue.

She pulled back to peer up at him, lashes dewy with unshed tears. He touched his finger to one of them, taking a teardrop onto his finger. "Or you let go of the thing that doesn't match up."

CHAPTER 21

After lunch Jones took Carol to more places on her written checklist.

"Should I be doing this?" Jones mused.

"Absolutely," Carol answered.

"Of course you think so. You're the enemy," he said.

"I'm not, though. The owners of the resort are the ones paying me to be here judging everything."

"But it seems disloyal to my fellow employees, some of whom may get in trouble when you turn in your report," he said.

"If they're doing their jobs, they have nothing to worry about."

He rolled his eyes. "Don't be such a goody-goody."

She jabbed him in the solar plexus, but she was smiling. "When a resort makes necessary improvements, it's a win for everybody. If some slackers have to be sacrificed for the good of the hotel, so be it."

"You're giving off solid Stalin vibes right now," he said.

They turned toward his bungalow to retrieve Ribs, but no need because he was headed right for them.

"You've got to be kidding me," Jones muttered when he saw who walked beside Ribs. Victoria Seymour, the woman who'd caught

Jones's interest the first time he met Carol, strode next to Ribs, deep in conversation.

"Of course the beautiful people would find each other," Carol said. "It's nature's law or something. Why is their lane so pretty?"

"How are they both in the cellulite-free lane?" Jones agreed.

"No halitosis in that lane, either. No adult-onset acne, muffin tops, male pattern balding, moles that grow hair," Carol added.

"Knees that don't pop when they stand from a crouch, never green food stuck between teeth," Jones continued.

"Never accidentally wear two different shoes with a run in the stockings," Carol picked up.

"Never go in for a hug when the woman goes in for a handshake so you end up grabbing something you shouldn't like an awkward perv," Jones said. Carol giggled. He smiled and they high fived.

"What's funny?" Ribs asked, eyes shifting between them.

"Swimming," Carol said and Jones snorted a laugh.

Victoria eased closer, entering Carol's personal space and engulfing her with the smell of expensive perfume. She leaned closer, squinting into Carol's face. "You are having makeup, no?"

"No. Yes?"

"You are not wearing makeup, yes?"

"Yes. No?"

She gathered a swath of Carol's long dress in her fist and held it aloft. "This dress is on purpose, yes? How you say, man repellent?"

Carol yanked the dress free. "It's intentional because I can roll it and it doesn't wrinkle. Is there a reason French Barbie is insulting me with a sophisticated accent?"

"I am not insulting. I am describing," Victoria said.

"I had an epiphany when I woke up," Ribs said.

"You realized it had been twelve hours since you had access to a blond woman?" Jones guessed.

"I realized that if Carol isn't the asset, the asset is still here." He made a little flourish toward Victoria.

"You have got to be kidding," Carol said. "You're a spy along with everything else?"

"What eez everything else?" Victoria asked, perfectly arranged features tipped toward the perfect angle to appear perfectly confused.

"Oy," Jones muttered, but he couldn't stop the hint of intrigue from leaking into his tone. Beautiful and a spy was his perfect combo, like catnip. Carol shot him a look and he shrugged. "I can admire the other lanes."

She rolled her eyes and faced forward. "How does this change anything?" she asked Ribs.

"They know a woman and man are their contact, not which woman and man. Victoria and I will do it, leaving you two off the hook," Ribs said.

On a personal level Jones felt mixed emotions—disappointment to still be out of the game, but relief for Carol's sake. Finally, she was safe. And then he saw her face. Arms crossed, eyes big, staring at Victoria in a way that made her thoughts obvious. And once again he saw her not as she was, but as she had been. The little girl who wasn't good enough to be included in her father's life. Before he could think it through, his emotions once again got him in trouble when he spoke.

"Yeah, that's not going to happen. Carol and I are taking point on this mission. You two will be our backup."

Jones and Ribs had known each other for nearly a decade. They'd served on countless missions together, spent untold hours of downtime learning each other's ins and outs, their strengths and weaknesses. Few times over that decade had Jones ever taken what his teammates liked to call The Tone. Usually he was easygoing and fun loving. But when The Tone arrived, they knew he meant it. And while Ribs might be surprised to hear The Tone deployed in this instance, he knew better than to argue.

Hands up in surrender, he gave a little nod of assent. "Your turf, Jonesie."

Victoria, who didn't share their long history, was baffled. "What? They are not capable of this assignment. He is a security guard. She is a civilian. This is too much to work with." Once again she held Carol's oversized dress in her hand, this time for Ribs's inspection.

Carol snatched it away. "If David says we're doing it, we're doing it."

She inched closer to Jones and, just like that, he and Gum Lady were a team.

✧

"*I* do not do well as backup," Victoria announced. For the third time since Jones decided he and Carol would run the op. He was still a bit fascinated by her. Clearly there was more to her than beauty, especially if she was a spy. On the other hand she was rather grating.

So is Carol, he reminded himself, except now it was hard to remember. Carol trucked along beside him, smiling a secret little smile like she'd recently learned they were on the way to her surprise birthday party. She hadn't said a word since he made his dramatic pronouncement, and that was a surprise. In his experience with Carol, she never seemed to miss an opportunity to express a contradictory opinion. On the other hand, if her phone was to be believed, everyone really did call her Sweetie. Maybe he did have it wrong. Maybe she was actually a nice person and he had received the world record for the worst first impression ever. And now Victoria, who he'd believed must be the epitome of perfection, was turning out to be a bit of a yammering harpy. All in all it was very confusing. He wished he could channel Ribs, who had formed some sort of dethatched amusement and was using it as a shield, sly glance bouncing between the two women and Jones like they were actors in some play. Maybe they were. Jones didn't know anymore.

What he did know was that he was now running this op, and it felt a bit like waking up after a long slumber. His body remembered this feeling of sharp adrenaline, even if his mind temporarily forgot. *All cylinders, Jones,* he told himself, stretching his neck and shoulders.

"Are you sore?" Carol asked, startling him from his reverie. She rested her hand on his bicep and stared up at him, brown eyes matching pools of warm concern. If he said yes, he somehow knew she'd try to do something about it. Give him medicine, a massage, warm compress or even food to ease his misery. He had no idea how he knew, but he knew: Carol was a nurturer. Something about that knowledge twisted his gut in a way that wasn't wholly unpleasant.

"No, I stretch before a mission. Usually they involve a lot of muscles that will be sore later if I don't loosen them up first," he explained.

"Maybe I should stretch, too," she suggested. She looked so adorably earnest and—excited?—that he didn't have the heart to tell her there was no need. He'd be doing the legwork, if any was needed. She was merely along for the ride. But he lacked the heart to burst her bubble, the one where she now envisioned herself as a pint-sized commando.

"Probably a good idea," he said gravely, purposely ignoring the way Ribs beamed at him behind her back. *Shaddup,* he wanted to tell Ribs, because he was reading things that weren't there. Wasn't he? It was the nice thing to do, to include her, and Jones was nice. Everyone agreed. It was kind of his thing. Mr. Nice Guy. And there was nothing wrong with that. Nothing at all.

"Odd, I have never stretched before a mission," Victoria inserted, looking lithe and limber like a professional ballerina.

"And what about you, Ribs?" Carol asked amicably, ignoring Victoria's veiled jibe, if that was what it had been. Jones wasn't well versed in the ways of women, but he knew enough to realize sometimes there could be a whole other world going on beneath the surface, like taking a microscope to a tide pool and realizing there was an entire universe of invisible things happening unaware.

"It doesn't matter if I stretch or not. Somehow I always end up sore now," Ribs returned in an equally amicable tone that for some reason annoyed Jones. It wasn't his job to placate people. That was what Jones was for. Except at the moment his mind was too busy with the mission, and that gave him a bit of an epiphany. Maybe the reason the guys counted on him to be the comic relief was because he was always free to do so, because he was never the one in charge. Being responsible for people's lives had a way of sucking the levity away.

Jones had rarely been in that position before. Usually he was along for the ride and it left his mind and emotions free for other things, for distraction, for cheering, for taking care of the emotional wellbeing of those who *were* in charge. But now this was his baby and he felt stressed and distracted, pressed by the weight of responsibility and, oh no, did he hate it? *Too late now,* he thought. Ribs would get to be Mr. Fun while Jones led the charge, stomping a little as his mind calculated what it would need to carry himself and Carol safely through the coming hours.

Overhead the wind picked up and the sun dropped behind a cloud and Jones realized a literal storm was nearing, too, adding another complication. As a navy guy he'd learned to calculate for wind, a sometimes cruel mistress for any sailor. Wind could be kind, pushing you gently in the direction you needed to go. Or wind could kill, flipping you off course and burying your location, along with your body. And now it would be a factor, one more thing to monitor on this island that lived and died by weather patterns.

He didn't realize he was scowling until Carol slipped her hand into his, giving it a reassuring squeeze. He glanced down at her. She smiled up at him and he smiled in return, the tension easing out of his features and shoulders. He took a deep breath, more of the tension draining away. Behind Carol Ribs beamed.

"Shaddup," Jones told him, out loud this time.

Ribs held up his hands in surrender again. "I didn't say a word."

He didn't have to. By now Jones knew him well enough to read his innuendo and faced forward, fighting a blush and feeling nostalgic for the protective safety of his office.

CHAPTER 22

His bungalow felt oddly cozy for a plotting session with Indonesian gangsters. Jones sat at the bar connected to the kitchen, idly listening while Ribs and Victoria swapped war stories. He could have added a few of his own, but he didn't. Not only was his mind occupied with the coming task, but it would have made him feel a little pathetic, like he was trying too hard to be one of them. And even though he had technically been an elite commando for a decade, he wasn't one of them, not really. Not only had he left that world behind but, at heart, maybe he had always been that Nebraska farm boy. And maybe that was okay.

The other source of the coziness, Carol, was currently filling the space with enticing smells. Jones had no idea what magic she wove, only that his house had never smelled like this before. Somehow it was as if the smells had transformative powers that replaced all the empty molecules, making the space feel lived in and alive, vibrant with spice and vitality. He tried to muster a bit of annoyance at the repeated interruptions but failed mightily. Jones was and always had been a people person. Despite how much he'd tried to keep his home separate from work, it now felt like heaven to have it populated by noise and life and a flow of humanity. Like the end of a dangling cord finally plugged back into a receptacle. After a few moments of pretending not to watch, he set aside his paper and rested his head on his arms, dozily watching Carol as she flitted around his kitchen.

"Like watching a cooking show," he murmured. She finished chopping whatever she'd been working on, tossed it into a hot pan with a satisfying sizzle, gave it a little shake, and tossed Jones a piece of banana. He caught it in his mouth like a dog and, with zero remorse, made a pathetic face, hoping for more.

"Wait, I have a thing," Carol said, giving the pan a shake again. Then from somewhere beneath the counter she removed an oversized green coconut and machete. That was so surprising that Victoria and Ribs paused their comparison of their time in Belarus to dart her a confused glance.

"Don't you love having these whenever you want them?" Carol gushed.

"Um…sure," Jones said cagily.

She paused hacking at the thing to frown. "David, really? You live in tropical paradise and you've never had a fresh coconut?"

"I've been busy," he defended, a blatant lie. The truth was that green coconuts were on the list marked OTHER. Coconuts should be brown, dried, and on a market shelf in America where he would similarly never touch them. "Why does it bother you?"

She paused, frowning now at the coconut. "I don't know. Maybe because I feel you're not living up to your potential."

"Maybe I am," Jones countered. "Maybe all there is to me is a guy who likes hot dogs and corn on repeat."

She set aside the coconut and leaned closer, resting her hands on the counter between them. "Then why are you here? Why didn't you stay in Nebraska? Why did you become a SEAL instead of remain a sailor? There's dignity in both those things. What drove you to seek the next step?"

The question gave him pause. "Because I wanted more," he said, but the answer wasn't good enough for Carol.

"Everyone wants more. Dig a little deeper. What was it that pushed you to those things specifically? Leaving home, attaining further training, moving to an island half a world away."

His heart thumped and he had no idea why, but it was the same sort of anticipation he'd felt when he read the ad for his current job. Why, though? What was the connection between all the things he'd pushed his life to become? It wasn't about escape, because he had neither wanted nor needed to escape. Jones loved his life, his family, his people. Leaving them had been the hardest part.

"I guess," he eked slowly, thoughts running ahead of his words as they attempted to align themselves in the proper order. "I guess I wasn't content to lead an ordinary life. I wanted to make certain my life was full, that I lived it to the utmost and the fullest, claiming every experience."

Carol beamed at him, a teacher whose star pupil had made her proud. "Exactly. Food is part of that; food is part of everything. To come all this way and not immerse yourself means you're missing a vital step in attaining the full experience." She finished arranging the coconut, inserted a giant straw she'd also miraculously procured, and presented it to Jones. Dutifully he took a sip. Carol clasped her hands under her chin, awaiting his reaction.

"Okay, it's amazing," he admitted.

Carol beamed and gave his arm a squeeze. "I knew there was more to you than met the eye, David." Satisfied, she busied herself once again with whatever was in the pan. Jones returned his attention to the coconut, feeling…things. Few people in his life had ever believed there was more to him than met the eye. Early on his friends had been content to see him as the obligatory fat kid, never realizing the heart of a warrior beat inside. Even after his transformation people stubbornly held on to the affable image. *Jones is so nice, so sweet, so even tempered and cheerful.* He was all of those things, and they were all good, positive things to be. What ate at Jones, what drove him and kept him up at night, was the unacknowledged *something more* inside him. And somehow Carol, painfully irritating, nitpicky *Carol,* was the one to see and recognize.

His glance slid to Victoria. If he were being honest, it was her recognition he'd been hoping for, or maybe someone like her. He had long wanted one of the beautiful others to look at him and see the hidden depths. The world described Victoria and women like her as a ten. She seemingly had it all. Jones had always believed that while the world might view him as a six, based on the exteriors, inside he was also a ten. Life, circumstance, and the judgment of others had incorrectly miscategorized him. But what if she did turn and see him? What if her blinders were miraculously removed and she was able to see inside him the way Carol was somehow able to see inside him? What then? Because for the last fifteen minutes she'd been talking about Eastern Europe and if she said Belarus one more time Jones thought he might hurl the coconut at her head.

On the other hand while Victoria blathered—to the point where even Ribs's eyes were glazed with boredom—Carol created some sort of good-smelling magic with a mishmash of exotic ingredients. *What if Carol is like me, too? What if she has hidden depths and realms no one would ever guess at and, like me, she's been waiting for someone to pause and peer inside, to unveil all the hidden wonders?*

Carol realized he was staring at her and paused, suddenly self-conscious. "What?"

"It smells really good," he mused.

She sliced him a bite of mango, holding it aloft. His hands were occupied by the coconut. Without thinking he opened his mouth and she dropped it inside. Maybe it was because the mango was fresh, or maybe everything tasted better when Carol fed him. Whatever the reason, it was the best bite of fruit he'd ever had.

"I've always wanted to feed a SEAL," Carol said.

Jones snorted a laugh, choking a little on a tiny hunk of mango. "You're pretty cute, Carol," he said when he could speak, then had the pleasure of watching a tiny little blush spill into her cheeks.

"You're not so bad yourself, David," she said softly, and tossed him another bite of fruit.

CHAPTER 23

Jones tried to plan, he really did. He sat at the table that night, long after Ribs, Carol, and Victoria retired, hand hovering over his notebook. When he finally took a hard look at what he'd put to paper he saw the word GUNS with a question mark, along with a pretty decent drawing of a mango and banana.

So maybe strategizing wasn't his strong suit.

Or maybe it was the fact that he was on a far-flung tropical island with limited backup, ammo, comms, and a civilian for a partner. When he thought about the weight of what he'd done—getting Carol into this mess and then sticking the landing by volunteering her to be their bait—he kind of wanted to pick her up and run away. To force carry her to somewhere safe. Because no matter how he spun it, what they were about to do was incredibly dangerous. And every time he tried to warn her about it, she shoved food into his mouth to make him stop talking. Or maybe she sincerely enjoyed shoving food in his mouth. Probably so, but not as much as he enjoyed eating it. He couldn't remember the name of what she made, something Thai, but it was hands down the best thing Jones ever tasted.

Thinking of it now made his stomach burble with desperate longing. With a quick peek to make certain he wasn't observed, he sneaked to the fridge and opened it, poking his head inside.

"Hungry?"

Jones spun, emitting the first sound that came to him. "Wamhoobie."

Carol stood behind him, wearing a nightshirt with a picture of a cartoon horse riding a motorcycle on it. "Did I startle you so badly you made up a new language?"

"No. I was…praying," Jones improvised.

"To Wamhoobie or for wamhoobie?"

"It's interchangeable. Like aloha," he explained, smiling when she laughed.

"But you are hungry," she clarified.

"I eat when I'm nervous," he said, tone slightly defensive. Emotional eating was always a sore subject for a former fat kid.

"Same. What did you find?"

He glanced into the fridge. "A frozen hot dog and some mayonnaise."

"As a chef, I'm afraid I can't let you eat that," she said, shaking her head sadly.

"On whose authority can you stop me?" he challenged.

"By the power of Auguste Escoffier," she said.

He closed the fridge and leaned on it. "I'm a highly decorated former Navy SEAL. What have you got?"

"Weaponized toque and bullet –proof apron," she replied. "Plus, you know, a lot of knife training."

"So, what, you're going to dice me into tiny pieces?"

"I prefer a nice julienne," she said, shrugging.

"Wow, I'm terrified. I guess there's nothing left for me but to surrender."

"Wise choice. And now I must complete the surrender ritual, in which I make you a delicious snack."

"Your enemies must be so confused," he said.

"And also well fed," she added.

"Impossible. I have no food here," he said.

"Ah, but you only think you have no food," she said, holding a finger aloft.

"I want to see the magic happen," he said, his tone holding a challenge.

She took a step forward and paused. "You have to say the magic word."

Between them his stomach gurgled loudly.

"Congratulations, you guessed it," she said, taking another step forward. The kitchen was tiny, too small for both of them. Jones skirted around her and resumed his seat at the counter. He earnestly didn't believe Carol could come up with anything in his empty, lackluster kitchen, but soon she began removing things and placing them on two plates. And when she slid his plate in front of him it looked like something from a photo shoot.

"How?" he said, pausing to stare at it before diving in. That was how he knew it was special, because he was able to pause before the coming gobble.

"The quintessential French kitchen is never without bread, butter, jam, cheese, and chocolate."

That was coincidentally what she'd arranged for him, a sliced baguette with butter, cheese, and jam and a frothy cup of warm chocolate. She settled her plate beside him and took the adjoining barstool. The silence was strangely companionable until she spoke.

"Why are you still up? Or are you some kind of night owl?"

"I was thinking, going over strategy."

"What's our strategy?" she asked.

He checked his notes: GUN, banana, mango. He faced her. "To not die."

She faced him, holding her chocolate aloft in a little salute. "Solid plan, I like it."

There wasn't space for both of their knees. Jones attempted to move aside to make room but soon gave up. Their knees touched now, pressed together like puppy noses. He hunched forward imploringly. "I'm serious here, Carol."

Carol hunched forward, too, mimicking him. "I know you are,

David. That's what makes it so wholesome." Her right hand set the empty chocolate cup on the counter. Her left hand slid onto his knee.

He stared down at it, thinking. When was the last time a woman touched him? Two years ago, Angelina Beckworth, a woman his mother set him up with. He had half-heartedly tried to like her, but instead his attention was diverted to a hot woman he met on social media, one who later turned out to be a Nigerian scammer. The other guys, Ribs, Ethan, Ridge when he was single, used to have stalkers. SEAL groupies who would seemingly do anything to marry a guy in special forces. Jones had been the guy they went to for an in with their pathetic antics. *You're so nice,* had been the resounding theme of his feedback from the female of the species. Guys he'd known could ignore a woman, cheat on her, forget her name, and still have women beating down their doors. Jones had always treated women kindly, with respect, like a queen. And he was *so nice!* Nice had come to represent something bad in his mind, so much that he'd become skittish and standoffish, admiring a woman from afar instead of forming any meaningful connection, afraid of the coming rejection.

Before he could think it through his hand lifted hers and brought it to his lips. Carol's lashes fluttered and Jones stared down at her fingers. He had never been that guy, the one with the moves his teammates seemed to naturally posses. In the past every time he'd attempted to ease out of the Friendzone with a woman, she'd eased him back in again. *David, you are SO NICE. And SO CUTE. I care about you SO MUCH, too much to ever date you. You're SUCH A GOOD FRIEND.* He had come to loathe those three words—nice, cute, and friend.

"What's the horse for?" he asked.

"In chess?" she asked, sounding a bit dazed.

"On your shirt." He pointed to her nightshirt, the horse riding a motorcycle.

She glanced down. "Horse power. It was from Brody. It made him laugh. He's very funny." In contrast to her words she sounded sad, or maybe pensive.

"Funny is good," Jones said mildly.

"Funny is excellent," Carol agreed softly.

His thumb brushed over her fingers. "Is it enough?"

"I…" she stared at their combined hands, a slight frown puckering her brow. Her attention shifted to the paper he'd used to strategize. "Let me see what you have here." Slowly she leaned closer, bringing her body in sharp relief with his as she reached for the paper. He caught a whiff of something sweet, something floral, something citrus. Whatever it was, it was a delightful and potent combination. It would have been more natural to lean away, but he didn't, instead allowing his nose to brush against her hair.

Carol sat upright and studied the paper in serious concentration a minute before turning it to face him. "This is an excellent banana."

"I guess I'm not so great at strategizing," he said.

"You're good at a lot of other things," she said, setting the paper aside.

He wanted to ask what those things were, but couldn't figure out how without sounding needy. Carol seemed to view him through a different lens, however, and it was one he liked because he thought maybe it was the real one, the one he liked best.

This time when his hand reached out, it caressed her head. She tilted her face, leaning it into his palm. "I'm sorry I hated you, in the beginning."

She smiled, her cheek pressing into his open hand. "It's okay, no one ever has before. It was kind of funny. Sorry I gave you such a hard time."

"I got you into a terrible mess, with my temper."

"I don't mind," Carol said.

"How can that be possible? This is really dangerous."

"It's an adventure. Nothing like this has ever happened to me before. Someday when I'm old and gray, it will make a good story, how I got snagged into international intrigue because some guy thought I was a spy."

Jones's brow puckered. Was that what he would eventually someday be in her life story? "Some guy?" He felt like he'd spent his entire life trying to be more than "some guy."

Carol, oblivious to his reaction, continued. "It's no Belarus, though. Apparently nothing can top that as a locale for shenanigans, if Victoria is to be believed."

"As someone who has been to Belarus, let me assure you that's not true," he said.

"Have you really?" Carol gasped.

"Yes," he said, laughing. "Honestly, there are lots better places. I have no idea why she got stuck on it."

"She made it sound interesting, I'll give her that."

"For the first forty minutes, maybe."

"Maybe it's not Belarus; maybe it's Victoria. Maybe the Victorias of the world can make anything sound interesting." She sat up, imitating Victoria's perfect posture and dismissive head tilt. "'And so I counted ze used coffee grounds, one by one, and named them. Zere was Geraldine, Ernest, Rodrigo…' You know she could tell that story and some man in the world somewhere would hang on every word." Carol rolled her eyes, which was a good thing because she missed Jones's flush. He couldn't seem to help it, though. Previously, until today, as a matter of fact, he had been that person, the one who would have been content to listen to Victoria talk about something nonsensical and insipid, if only to use the opportunity to bask in her glorious presence. Seen through Carol's eyes, it seemed as silly and shallow as she described. Why should he waste his time dying for the attention of women who didn't want to give him the time of day or, worse, would use him and toss him away again?

"I've seen women do the same to Ribs," Jones said, somewhat defensively.

"I feel a little sorry for him," Carol surprised him by saying.

Jones blinked at her, shocked. "Why?"

"He's sad."

"What makes you think that?" He didn't believe her, he was merely curious. Ribs wasn't sad. The two of them were tight. If something was bothering Ribs, he'd open up and confess, Jones was certain. Wouldn't he? Because he knew Jones was there for him, would move heaven and earth to help. Or did he know that? Had Jones ever said as much?

"It's his eyes. There's some kind of sadness there. Not despair or depression, just something bothering him that's making him sad." As if echoing that sadness, Carol's lip jutted slightly as she stared at the counter, thinking.

"What about Victoria? Is she sad?"

"Victoria's a shark," she answered definitively. "Sharks don't feel sad. They feel hungry or not hungry. Victoria is hungry, very, very hungry."

"How do you know these things?"

"The eyes are the window to the soul. I've spent a lot of my life looking in windows, I guess."

"What about my eyes? What do they tell you?" He tipped his head, awaiting her inspection. She leaned closer and he caught a whiff of whatever good smelling thing was on her. Whatever it was, he liked it. The thing that frustrated him about Carol was that he couldn't easily identify the feelings she gave him. It wasn't lust, that much he was certain. It felt more precious than that, a tiny flame in need of nurture and protection. But what would be the point of a flame? It could only be doused when she went away. Jones wasn't certain exactly what he was looking for, but he knew what he wasn't, and that definitely included someone unreachable and far away.

When Carol took both his hands in hers, it was hard to remember. The little flame burst to life, spreading from his fingers to all the other parts of him, calling him to action. He needed to…to what? What was the thing all his molecules wanted him to do whenever he was near her? He didn't understand, and that lack of understanding left him frustrated and wanting.

Carol tipped her head and leaned in, studying him from very close by. Jones sat perfectly still, afraid to disrupt the moment, hoping an answer would come to him about what to do next, until he waited too long and she sat back, letting go of his hands.

"Your eyes try too hard to hide the truth of who you are," Carol said.

"You sound like a gypsy. What does that mean?"

"It means there is more to you than people realize, much more, but you keep it hidden."

"Why?" he asked, heart thumping with the truth of it. Was he so transparent? How did she know such things?

"You tell me," she urged.

"I guess if you don't put yourself out there, you don't get rejected," he said.

"Rejection is painful," Carol agreed.

He wondered if she was thinking of her father just then. They had this unfortunate thing in common, and maybe that was the thing Jones couldn't put a name to. They shared a sympathetic understanding, each realizing what it meant to be pushed away and disregarded. In Jones's case, he'd taken all his former fat kid angst and turned it around, becoming a fit Navy SEAL with an enviable pedigree. He wondered what Carol did with her rejection.

"You know what I think?" he blurted.

Carol's answering smile became wry. "What?"

"I don't think you're as nice as you pretend."

"Of course I am," she argued.

"No. I think you want to be nice, you try to be nice, but deep down you're kind of a troublesome spitfire. Much more like Gum Lady than Sweetie."

"People don't like troublesome spitfires. *You* didn't like the troublesome spitfire."

"Maybe I was wrong. And maybe you grew on me. And maybe you made me laugh, when you weren't making me crazy," he said.

Her nose wrinkled and her arms crossed over her chest. "That was an awful lot of maybes, David."

He touched his finger to her wrinkled, turned up nose. "You're pretty cute, Carol. And I didn't say maybe."

"What about you?" she countered.

He smiled. "Am I cute?"

"You know you are," she returned, reaching out to boop his button nose, too. "If I'm going to lean away from the niceness, you have to lean into it. Stop fighting it. You're not some macho meathead. Face it, you're *nice*."

"You take that back," he said, pressing his hands over his ears.

"No, because I love it. Too few people are genuinely kind in the world. Why would you pretend to be anything else?"

"It feels like I should be so much more, like I should be the hero."

"Someone who can take what the world dishes and remain soft-hearted *is* a hero."

"I'm not sure I believe you," he said. On the other hand it would be a relief to stop fighting it, to stop pretending to be someone he wasn't. So he was a nice guy. And women like Victoria didn't want nice. There were other kinds of women in the world, women like Carol, for instance, who saw the value in niceness.

"You should. I'm always right," she told him.

"What if I unleash the full power of my niceness and it doesn't work out? What then, Carol?" He was half-teasing, half sincere. How much rejection could a person take in a lifetime?

"Then we run away to Belarus and start over," she declared, tone solemn, and it was so unexpected he guffawed and pulled her into a hug, pressing his mouth to her shoulder to stifle it.

Carol returned his hug, resting her head on his shoulder as her arms circled his waist. "David."

"Yes, Carol." His head tipped, resting on hers, and it was nice. Cozy, but also that something else, that little unnamed spark that made him feel sort of fizzy and disoriented ever since they met.

"It's nice to be nice," she said.

"It's going well so far," he agreed, closing his eyes and breathing deeply. Why *did* she smell so good? Was it the food? Her skin? Some kind of lotion he could buy and keep on his nightstand for sniffing emergencies?

She eased back slightly. Her face was near his and slightly tipped to make her inspection. "I should...I should go to bed."

It felt natural for his hand to cup her face, his thumb skimming her throat. Carol was adorable, and that was how Jones responded to her, as if she should be adored. "I should..." he began, but had no idea how to continue because he had no idea what to do in the moment. He felt as though he stood on one side of a chasm. On the other side was the next place he needed to go, but he couldn't see it, and he had no idea how to get there. So he remained standing at the edge, peering over.

Carol paused, as if waiting for him to continue, to take the next step. When it became clear he either couldn't or wouldn't, she tipped forward and kissed his cheek, a soft skim of full lips that left him fighting a full-body shudder. "Good night, David," she whispered, breath blowing warm in his ear.

"Carol, wait," he whispered, but too late. By the time he opened his eyes and reached out a beseeching hand, she was already gone.

"I do not like to work with civilians," Victoria declared. Jones wasn't certain if her accent made everything sound moody and imperious or if she actually was those things. Whatever the reason, he never thought he'd be so glad to find some space away from such a beautiful woman.

"So you mentioned," he said dryly, tossing Ribs a conspiratorial glance that was lost on him. Ribs looked somber and deep in thought, harkening him back to Carol's earlier pronouncement. Was Ribs sad? If so, why?

"She is not ready," Victoria continued, talking about Carol as if she weren't standing right beside them, looking small and helpless and, if Jones would admit, not ready.

But at Victoria's declaration her face took on a mutinous pout and she puffed up, an angry little hen now. "Anything to add, Carol?" Jones prompted, tossing her a knowing look. *Do it,* he mentally urged. *Go full Gum Lady on her, let her have it.*

Carol's smile was sickly sweet and she smoothed a hand over her hair, as if physically pushing back the impulse to snap. "Of course not, David. Because that wouldn't be nice."

"And you arc *so nice,* Sweetie," he countered, heavy on the sarcasm.

"I have to be in order to counteract your toxic masculinity, David," Carol returned, still in the saccharine tone.

Ribs gave them a paternal smile, one that said he didn't understand what they were talking about, but approved anyway.

Jones poked Carol. "The looming explosion is going to be epic. I'm bringing popcorn for when you finally go postal."

"And what should I bring for when you finally go full romantic pussycat?" she asked, and Ribs snorted.

"Full romantic pussycat. I have to write that down to relay to the guys. Anyone have a pen?"

"Or possibly a plan?" Victoria inserted, tone frosty. "You may be content to enter this disaster with clever quips and longing glances, but I have a reputation for excellence to maintain. I will not fail this mission and you are in charge." Her finger jutted accusingly toward Jones's chest, but it was Carol who whirled on her, hands on hips.

"Then why did you miss your check in?" she demanded.

"What?" Victoria asked, blinking at her.

"We're in this mess partly because you missed your check in, meaning David's friend had to ask him to intervene and make contact. Where were *you* when you were supposed to be doing your job?"

Ribs blinked at her in surprise because it was the first time he'd heard her whip out the Gum Lady tone. Jones beamed in delight. He'd sort of missed the insufferable shrew, especially when it was being used in his defense instead of against him.

"I do not answer to you," Victoria said haughtily.

"Then neither do we answer to you. If David says he has it covered, then he has it covered. I'm certain he'll ask for your input if or when he needs it."

Victoria whipped around and stalked ahead of them, her high heels clicking angrily on the cobblestone

"Dang, Carol," Ribs said, impressed. "Are you sure you're not one of us? That was terrifying." He made a show of dabbing his forehead.

"I guess I'm a tad protective of my friends," Carol said.

"I guess we're lucky you're on our side. Also that you don't have access to weapons," Ribs said.

He was smiling but Jones, newly attuned to his expression, realized it didn't quite meet his eyes. Was Ribs sad? He couldn't ask in front of Carol. If his friend had any hope of confiding in him, he wouldn't do it in front of someone else.

"I tried to tell you," he said. "She's a killer."

"I'm not though," Carol said, blushing. "I think it's you, David. I think you bring out this side of me."

"He has that effect. Our SEAL team was a bunch of softies until Jones came along and made us fighters," Ribs said, giving Jones a half-hearted shoulder punch that still managed to hurt. Not that he let his wince show.

"I really am the wind beneath your wings," Jones agreed.

"Seriously, though, what is the plan here?" Ribs asked, eyebrow quirked in that way he always did before a mission, a signal that the time for fun was over and you'd better not be standing in his way because things were about to go down. Jones was intimidated by that look. It took him back to being the team's little brother, the funny fat kid, the one who couldn't be taken seriously as an actual threat.

"Well," he began. If he had a collar, he'd be tugging it.

"The plan is to not die," Carol said firmly, giving Ribs the hard stare.

He put up his hands and took a step back. "Sounds good. I suggest we follow it." Picking up the pace, he caught up with Victoria.

"Dang, Carol," Jones whispered after Ribs left them. "You actually are terrifying. Maybe you should join up, become a SEAL."

"Boats make me seasick. Besides, it would probably only work if I had a vested interest."

"Like someone picking on your friends?" he suggested.

"Is that what we are?" Carol asked, pausing mid-stride.

She stared up at him, blinking, waiting for his answer. Was she asking if they were still enemies or if they were more than friends? He felt like he was supposed to do something or say something or be something momentous, but as with everything lately he had no idea what that should be. So after an awkward pause he slowly replied, "I guess until something changes."

"Okay," she answered, a worrisome little pucker between her brows. It did something to him, that pucker, knocked something loose. Before she could take a step away, he put out a hand, grasping her forearm to hold her back.

"The thing is, Carol, that I have...I... Carol, the thing is... Here's the thing... The thing is that I have..." He could not plausibly figure out how to tell this woman he had a crush on her, or at least that was what he thought it was. Worse than his inability to speak was the fact that his stuttering had caught the attention of Ribs, who now stood behind Carol pressing the first two fingers of both hands together and making kissy motions with his lips. Carol started to swivel in his direction and Jones yanked her back. What was more humiliating, that his longtime friend thought he needed pointers on talking to a woman, or that he actually needed pointers on talking to a woman? They were both bad, and he didn't want Carol to see.

She stared up at him inquisitively, warm brown eyes like liquid chocolate over her adorable little pug nose. Had she gotten cuter, or was he only noticing it more since the loathing wore away?

He gave his head a little shake, pulling himself back in the game. *I can do this. I can totally do this.* "Carol, the thing is that I have a..." *Be a man. Do it. Say it. I like you, Carol. Those four words. Say them in that order.*

His mouth opened, but no further sound came out.

Carol took a little step forward and hooked her index fingers in two of his belt loops. "David, you saw me with a wad of gum in my hair, and then you saw my towel slip at the massage."

Don't nod, whatever you do, do not nod. And stop remembering the spa incident because it's seriously not helping your concentration.

"I guess what I'm saying is that we've breached deeper levels of humiliation with each other. You can say anything to me, absolutely anything, with no judgment. I promise." She took a tiny step closer, one that prompted him to put his hand on her waist. Behind her, Ribs pumped his fist encouragingly.

"The thing is that I have a..." a flash of motion caught his attention. "Gun."

Carol's lashes fluttered. "I know, you used it in the car the other day. I don't know a lot about them, but it seemed nice enough." She gave his chest a reassuring little pat.

"Gun," Jones said again, yelling and pointing this time before diving on top of Carol and rolling her aside.

From the corner of his eye he saw Ribs dive, and then the shot rang out.

☙

They hit the ground with the force of a cannon. Jones tried to take the impact as he rolled, but Carol made an "oomph" sound, as if the wind had been knocked from her. His gun was already out, but he remained immobile, Carol tucked safely beneath him. It was likely he was crushing her, but he couldn't ponder that now.

To his left Ribs was in a defensive crouch behind an oversized planter. Jones gave him raised eyebrows. *You got anything?*

Ribs shook his head in return, mouthing, *Victoria?*

Jones shrugged. He had no idea where the woman had disappeared to. He didn't see a body lying about. He would need to go investigate, but he didn't want to leave Carol until he was certain she wasn't exposed.

"What happened?" she said, breathless. Whether that was from shock or the weight of him, he had no idea. He thought maybe the latter when he raised himself on his forearms and she sucked air.

"There was a shooter." He glanced down at her, assessing, and lingered. He'd heard the guys talk about how adrenaline could mix with testosterone to create a potent combo. He thought it was merely talk, but now he got it because with Carol pressed beneath him, all big-eyed and soft, he felt kind of like a cartoon wolf, tongue lolling, heart palpitating wildly, in desperate need of pursuit.

"Are you okay?" Carol asked. Her hand eked out of its cage and softly caressed his head.

"Yes. How about you? Are you smooshed? Did I break you when we tumbled?"

"No, I kind of enjoyed it," Carol replied.

"You are in desperate need of adventure, woman, if being tackled is your idea of fun," he said.

"Maybe it's not the fall so much as the person who fells you," she suggested.

It took him a second to process that, and then someone stood over them, casting an aggressively long shadow.

"He got away," Victoria said. Her voice was full of condemnation, or that was how Jones took it. They glanced up at her, squinting. The sun was high and directly behind her back.

"Did you get a look?" Jones asked. He rolled off Carol and put down a hand, helping her up. She tried to tidy all the dusty places, using her hand to brush herself and then Jones.

"He looked like a local. I have no idea if it was my contact, but it confirms what I earlier believed. *I* must be the one to make contact and complete the mission."

Reluctantly, Jones agreed. With the appearance of a shooter, his mind confirmed what his gut had been trying to tell him. This mission was too dangerous for Carol. He couldn't take any more chances with her safety, whether she wanted to or not.

"You can't," Carol declared.

At this point everyone seemed prepared to argue with her, but she pointed toward Victoria and continued. "You've been shot."

CHAPTER 25

"Who responds to being shot like that?" Carol declared, annoyed as they paced the resort's medical clinic, waiting for Victoria to be patched. "Seriously, she glances down at her arm with a tiny pout and says, *I do not have time for zis*, and didn't even get blood on her shirt. What is wrong with her? Is she even human? Is she a cyborg?"

Jones watched her pace back and forth, trying to wrap his mind around her annoyance. Nearby Ribs seemed intent on helping fuel it.

"Don't forget she ran after the guy in heels," he added.

Carol pointed at him. "Don't think I didn't factor that in. There is something seriously wrong with her." Now that she faced them, she encompassed them in her disapproving frown.

"What did we do?" Jones asked. His stomach gurgled, with hunger or nerves? He had no idea, but it didn't matter. He had already ascertained that there was no food in the medical clinic. Carol, attuned to the sound, reached in her purse and handed him a piece of cheese, mindlessly, as if on rote. Someone makes a hunger noise, she automatically provides sustenance. Magic.

"You're just *men*," she said, placing the cheese in his palm, along with two dried apricots that appeared as if by magic. "That's what you go for, all of you, blond and beautiful and oh-so-capable, and it was a busy morning, and I am so tired." She sat with a little harrumph, crossing her arms over her chest.

"Not all of us go for women like that," Ribs said mildly, but they both ignored him because of course men like Ribs went for women like Victoria. They were in the same lane; their destiny had already been established. So it was up to Jones to swallow his snack, sit next to Carol, and hold her hand.

She let out a pent up breath and rested her head on his shoulder with a murmured, "Sorry."

"You're hangry," he guessed.

"Maybe," she conceded, reaching into her purse for her own cheese/apricot snack.

"And tired," he added.

"A little."

"And stressed about everything that's been happening," he added.

"Surprisingly no," she said, and she sounded sincere.

"How can that be? I'm stressed," he said.

She fed him another apricot. "Sometimes you know a thing is the right thing to do. That's how I feel about this meeting. Information needs to be obtained, you need me to obtain it. Seems easy."

"But the danger," he said, after he swallowed his apricot.

"Danger, schmanger," Carol said.

"You worry me, Carol," he said.

In answer, she linked her arm with his and rested her head on his shoulder again, and it was *nice*. Jones felt the feeling again, the one he couldn't identify. The inability to put a name to it was driving him crazy. If he could figure out what it was, he might know what to do with it. In lieu of an answer, he shifted and kissed the top of her head. And though he couldn't see her, he could tell she smiled. That made him smile, which in turn made Ribs smile.

By the time the clinic's assistant came to retrieve them, they were all smiling like fools, probably the incorrect reaction to a teammate who'd just been shot. But Victoria was fine, they'd been assured of that when they brought her in, fully conscious and completely irritated. The bullet had merely grazed her arm, how badly remained to be seen.

"She's ready," the clinic's doctor said. Jones didn't think he was actually a doctor, but he obviously had some medical knowledge and ability to perform stitches. "The bullet grazed the muscle. She'll be sore and out of commission for a couple of days, but I expect it to heal nicely." He bit into a papaya, letting the juice flow freely down his chin, as if he needed to prove to them all how unconventional he was. Or maybe he was merely ready for them to go. The most he usually dealt with was resort guests with a hangover or sniffles. Whatever his reasoning, he abandoned Victoria into their care and disappeared.

Victoria emerged from the room next, looking crankier than before she went in. "Zat man got papaya juice on my dress." Her eyes narrowed on the doctor's retreating backside. If Jones were him, he'd watch his back the next few days until she was over her snit.

"Are you okay?" Carol asked.

Victoria seemed confused. "Yes, why wouldn't I be?"

"Because a gun shot a bullet through your body," Carol said slowly.

"Bah, was a graze," Victoria said, waving her away with the free hand on her good arm, her left.

"But can you shoot?" Ribs interjected.

Victoria paused, and they had their answer. Her breath left in a defeated little sigh. "I am not as good as I would like with my left."

Carol rubbed her temples. Jones didn't need her thoughts to understand them this time. *That's what makes her feel bad about herself? That she's not as good at killing people with her left hand as she is with her right? What is wrong with this woman?* Out loud she said, "That settles it, then. We're back to the original plan. David and I will have the meeting and retrieve the information."

Victoria and Ribs shared a significant look. Neither was comfortable with the idea, but with Victoria out of commission, it had moved from novel to necessary.

No one said anything, and Carol took their silence personally. She sat up away from Jones. "Come on, you guys, it will be fine. We're not going on a mission. We're taking a meeting. I've taken dozens of meetings over the years. I'm quite good at receiving information. Like a human answering machine."

"Okay," Ribs said, moving away from the wall he'd been keeping upright. "Let's do this. Victoria and I will run comms and be backup. You two will take the meeting."

"We're ready. Put us in," Carol demanded cheerfully. "Right, David?" She turned to peer up at Jones, and it happened again. His stomach clenched painfully and turned over because…because why?

His face must have been expressive because Ribs said, "Yes, David, are you ready?"

"I…okay," Jones stammered.

Victoria huffed, and everyone faced her. "Zis, then, is the best the American office has to offer. Explains a lot." With a swish of her perfect blond hair, she turned and stormed out of the clinic.

"Are we certain she wasn't the intended target? Like someone who knows her personally was trying to take her out, maybe," Carol suggested.

"No way," Ribs said. "If it was personal against her, they definitely wouldn't have missed."

"I know we're new friends, but I really love you," Carol declared, beaming at him.

"There's a lot of that going around in this room," Ribs agreed. He tossed Jones a significant look, and Jones shook his head. Clearly he was attracted to Carol, but he didn't love her. He barely knew her. "Why don't you go on ahead? Jones and I need to talk about…strategy."

"I'll go catch up with Victoria. I think our plan to become lifelong besties is really coming along," Carol said as she exited the clinic.

Ribs watched her go with a smile. "She's adorable. All pint-sized and sassy. Like sweet and sour sauce in one of those plastic bear containers."

"That is so genuinely weird," Jones replied.

"No, what's weird is watching your reaction to her," Ribs said.

"What do you mean?" Jones asked, squirming a little.

"First you hated her. I've known you ten years and not seen you hate anyone before, not even insurgents. So it was pretty funny to see you hate someone named Sweetie who is five feet tall and supplies you with sugar on the regular. But now my amusement has morphed into genuine concern."

Jones pinched the bridge of his nose. "Look, I know I screwed up. I got her into this ordeal and am probably the first person in the history of ever to confuse the Culinary Institute of America with the actual CIA," here he paused for Ribs's snort of amusement. "But I can't shake her. She's determined to see the assignment through, for whatever reason."

"Jones, it's not about the mission," Ribs exclaimed.

"Then what is it about?" Jones asked.

"Your fear. Your absolute terror over the thought of being attracted to Carol, your complete and utter incompetence when it comes to wooing her, and your stubborn refusal to make a move."

Jones stared at him, perplexed. "Are you...are you giving me love advice?"

"I'm trying," Ribs said.

"Why?"

"Because you need it. Because I care. Because you're one of my best friends and I had no idea you were this hopelessly bad at it."

"Why does it matter? I barely know her. What I do know drives me kind of crazy. She's temporary, and she has a boyfriend."

"When's the last time you met a woman who made you feel the way she makes you feel?" Ribs countered.

"I..." his words trailed helplessly away. Never. The answer was never. No one in his entire life had made him feel the full range of emotions Carol evoked in him. No one as angry, as frustrated, as intrigued, as protective. Surely that wasn't love, though. "I just met her," he said weakly.

"Sometimes, Jones, that's all it takes. Sometimes you can glimpse a woman in a window for five seconds and spend the rest of your life loving only her."

He sounded so certain, and so...haunted. "Gaines, are you okay?"

The use of his given name made him snap back into focus with a little shake of his head. "What? Yes, obviously. This isn't about me, it's about you. All I'm saying is to be open to the possibility of something more, even if it makes no sense on paper. And for the love of all that is good, man, *make a move.* I'm not certain how clearer Carol could be with her signals. Five more minutes and *I* was about to kiss her."

"You think she *wants* me to make a move?" Jones choked.

"She couldn't be any clearer if she wrote it with sparklers and hired a skywriter."

"That would be less clear, actually," Jones said vaguely. Did Carol actually want something to happen between them? "What about the boyfriend?"

"That's probably a question for Carol instead of me," Ribs said.

"I thought you were the one with all the answers," Jones said.

"Jonesie, I have nothing but hopes and dreams for your happiness, man." He thumped his fist over his heart a couple of times.

"I'll think about it," Jones replied.

"Two more words and then I'm done: carpe diem."

It wasn't seizing the moment Jones feared, it was the three words that usually came after: crash and burn. In Jones's experience guys like Ribs could get away with the big moments, the brave stunts and grand romantic gestures. They never seemed to work out for guys like Jones, fading instead to unending awkwardness. Although with Carol there would be no lingering awkwardness because she was going away. *What do I have to lose?* Or perhaps a better question, *what do I have to gain?*

CHAPTER 26

Jones still had to do his job, despite his involvement with Carol, Ribs, and their more interesting case. Victoria went wherever pretty people go to pout, and Carol volunteered to teach Ribs to cook an omelet. Reluctantly Jones tore himself away from the sight of them laughing and cracking eggs in his kitchen in order to walk across the resort grounds and closet himself in his office.

Not much had happened in his absence, and he wasn't certain how to feel about that. On the one hand his job felt boring and unimportant in light of the bigger case. On the other hand it was nice to grab a moment of peace and take a deep breath. The temptation was always there to follow Ribs not only back to the states but back to his former life. He could easily become a spy. He could take the same dashing and heroic assignments his friends took, travel the country, max out on lost sleep, never know where he was going to lay his head on any given night. But he had consciously chosen a path that ran contrary to that life.

Why?

Because I want a home and family someday. I want a wife and children. I want to be an active part of their daily lives, to live long enough to see them grown up.

As he sat in his office, skimming incident reports about drunken guests, he had no regrets about the hard choice he had made. It was right to walk away from a life of danger for something soft that paid well. After a few years at this job, he'd be able to retire comfortably and look for something 9-5 that would allow him to be the kind of family man he longed to be. The problem wasn't his job; the problem was the family portion of that equation.

His mind and heart agreed he'd made the right career choice, but both shrugged when he tried to bring up the other half of his pending future. Who would his wife be? How could he be there for a family that didn't yet exist? Somehow it had seemed so easy in theory: find a woman and make babies. In reality Jones felt confused and flustered when presented with the reality. How *did* people meet and fall in love? Who was he supposed to marry and why?

Previous to Victoria's arrival he would have said she was his ideal woman. Someone equally beautiful and brave. But Victoria was horrid. What if everyone who looked that good on the outside was equally bad on the inside?

Not possible, Jones told himself, giving his head a little shake. Certainly there were plenty of beautiful people who were kind and lovely. But how would Jones ever meet them, secreted away on his island as he was? And what of Carol?

His heart gave a painful little flop at the thought of her, both of her presence and the possibility of her going away. He had a solid life plan: get a well-paying job, retire early, have family. Nowhere in the plan was "meet woman who makes you crazy." She was a step out of time, something unforeseen, and he had no idea what to do with her.

Someone tapped on his door, making him realize he'd been staring vaguely into space, thinking about Carol, when he was supposed to be working.

"Come in," he said.

Lucinda poked her head in, a plate of donuts held aloft like a sacrificial offering. "Fresh from the fryer."

"Oh, my heart," Jones replied, not sure if he meant it literally or metaphorically. It was sort of amazing that two women now fed him,

Lucinda with the pastries and Carol with all the adventurous food he'd formerly been too skittish to sample. On the other hand the steaming pile of sugar fried dough really couldn't be great for his cardiovascular system.

Lucinda beamed and set the plate on his desk. He studied her, thinking of Carol's words as he did so. *You should ask her out, she likes you.* Did she? And should he? She was cute, with her dark skin and curly hair, a local who perfected her English by going stateside for college. He opened his mouth but, as with Carol, no sound came out. He couldn't make himself utter the words. *Lucinda, would you like to grab coffee sometime?* They were easy enough to say but, unlike with Carol, he wasn't afraid to say them. Rather he wasn't certain he wanted to. What was wrong with him? Lucinda was cute, Lucinda fed him, Lucinda was *available*, and Jones couldn't muster so much as a palpitation for her. It was so aggravating he was accidentally scowling when she set down the platter and looked at him.

She froze. "You know, don't you?"

Now his heart was staccato because what did he know? Or what was he supposed to know that he didn't? "Um...which what do I know?"

"That a spy is here," Lucinda said, dropping her voice to a conspiratorial whisper.

"Um..." He swallowed hard and took a breath. "A spy?"

She nodded. "A hotel spy, sent here by corporate to judge us and report back to them."

"Oh," he drawled, relieved. "How did you hear about that?"

"Manny."

Manny, her uncle, was the resort's manager. It occurred to Jones that he had the most to lose out on by Carol's presence and pending report. If she noted too much going wrong or in need of change, Manny might find himself unemployed. He wondered, but didn't ask, how Manny learned his information.

"I think I know who it is," Lucinda continued, still in the whisper.

"Who?"

"That blond lady with the French accent. She's horrible, and her manner makes me suspicious."

Jones stuffed a donut in his mouth so he wouldn't laugh. The actual spy had been found out. Meanwhile the fake spy, Carol, had been roped into doing real spy work. *What a tangled web we weave...*

"Better keep her happy, then," Jones said after he'd swallowed.

"Impossible," Lucinda sniffed, her pleasant accent making a return with her displeasure. "And everyone is on to her because she's been snooping around, asking questions."

"What kinds of questions?" Jones asked.

"Like kinds of things people smuggle off the island," Lucinda said. "Not the staff, of course, but she went to the bar with some of the locals, let them buy her drinks, and began asking questions."

"What would smuggling have to do with the resort?" Jones asked.

"Clearly she thinks the resort is a front for smuggling, and if that is happening then someone is not doing his job well, yes?" Lucinda's brows rose in anticipation of Jones's answer. He paused before he gave it, thinking. The conversation had taken an odd turn. All of a sudden he wasn't certain if Lucinda had come to bestow gossip or try and get some. And if she wanted information, was it for herself or her uncle, the resort's manager? *Who knew there'd be this much intrigue at a tropical resort?*

"What is the weather up to out there?" he asked, diverting to a safer topic.

"Bah, nothing good," Lucinda said, waving her hand. "Once again they were wrong in their prediction for us. My grandfather says we will take a direct hit."

"Already I know enough to trust your grandfather over a scientist. I guess we can be thankful it's a tropical storm and not a hurricane. I should do some rounds, make certain our backup power and emergency prep are up and running." He checked on those things weekly, as part of his routine, but suddenly he had the desire to make Lucinda go away. She made him uncomfortable, and he couldn't put his finger on why.

"I'm certain you'll find everything in order," Lucinda replied. She lingered awkwardly.

"Thanks for these," Jones tried. He tapped the plate she'd delivered, but somehow he'd lost his appetite for them, after only eating one.

"You're welcome," she said and finally took her leave.

Jones remained staring at the door a long time after she was gone, thinking. Was whatever intel he and Carol were about to receive in regard to smuggling? And, if so, what would it be? The island was a hotspot for drugs, caught as it was between Indonesia and the ocean. Money laundering was a possibility, but there were other things people tried to sell, namely wildlife and plants. Jones had been shocked to realize there was a big illegal market for kidnapped monkeys, stolen fish, and birds. Millions of dollars changed hands on a daily basis here, for anything and everything contraband. The Chinese wanted shark fins, the Japanese wanted plants, the Americans wanted animals, the Russians wanted minerals. It seemed everyone wanted something and would be willing to pay impossibly large sums, if the goods were illicit enough.

Outside thunder rumbled, stealing Jones's attention. His head swiveled toward the sound, too far to be startling but ominous enough to create some low-level anxiety about what was to come. A storm would be the perfect cover for smugglers. This would be Jones's second big storm since his arrival at the resort. He knew from experience everyone battened down the hatches and headed inside. Last time he'd gone on patrol during the storm and the place had resembled a ghost town. On a neighboring island a roaming gang of thieves had used the opportunity to steal over a hundred catalytic converters from the resort's fleet of cars, vans, and trucks. If his resort was somehow connected to a smuggling ring, the pending downtime would be the ideal moment to make a move.

Maybe it's time I took a second look at the resort, he thought, pushing aside the plate of donuts and heading for the door.

CHAPTER 27

Maybe it was his imagination, but Jones felt everyone's eyes on him as he strode through the resort for his rounds.

"Hey, Boss." One of the café workers, Marcus, greeted him with a smile and upraised nod. Jones almost answered back with his standard greeting, *I'm no one's boss,* and paused. Though it was true that he only had a few direct employees beneath him, he was senior management. Now, thanks to Carol, he began to feel the weight of it. Previously he had felt a sort of detached amusement toward the resort, exactly like someone who was putting in his time and would someday be free. But now he felt some ownership, some responsibility to make the place perfect and amazing, if only because guests were paying enough to make it so. The reputation was a five-star resort. Did it currently live up to that standard?

"Marcus," Jones greeted him and beckoned him closer. "Why is there a wet floor sign out?"

Marcus stared at the sign, scratching his head. "Because the floor is wet."

"Why is the floor wet?"

"Because Janine mopped."

"Why did Janine mop in the daytime when all cleaning of public spaces is supposed to be done at night?"

"Um…" Marcus looked cornered, not wanting to rat on Janine, but also not wanting to implicate himself in any sort of trouble.

"Never mind. Will you please put the sign away and then tell Manny I want to talk to him." If something nefarious was happening in the resort, Manny would know. Though not overtly energetic when it came to work, he had his finger on the pulse of everything, including all the juicy or scandalous gossip.

"Will do," Marcus said, now giving Jones a wide berth and a wary side eye.

There was a not-so-small part of Jones that wanted to hail him back, to laugh it off and explain he was having a bad moment, a stressful morning. But the other, bigger part of him understood that it was time to step up and assert himself. As a senior staff member of the resort, it was up to him to make certain everything ran smoothly.

Blast Carol, he thought, but couldn't seem to muster any anger. Instead he felt a strange sort of thankfulness. Something had been out of place and off since he began his new job. Previously he had chalked it up to being far from home and away from his comfort zone in the military, but what if it was more? What if, as Carol and Ribs both pointed out, it was time for him to take a stand and stop being so passive? In every area of his life.

He had no idea he was heading toward his bungalow until he pushed open the door and stepped inside. And then he paused on the threshold and inhaled. It smelled amazing. Somehow with Carol there it even felt different. More alive, more like home, more like *his.*

Her head whirled at the sound, beaming a smile in his direction over her shoulder. "Hiya."

Jones froze in the open doorway, feelings flowing out of him like runaway horses. He tried to capture one and ask it its name, but it got away. Instead he remained immobile, attempting to orient himself. His hand gripped the handle in an effort to regain his equilibrium. All he seemed able to grasp was that Carol was here, and maybe the absolute rightness of that threw him. "Hi," he croaked.

"Taste this," she commanded.

"I just had a don…" he started, but too late because she was already shoving something between his lips. Whatever it was contained some sort of sticky syrup that coated her finger. He licked it before she could take it away, and now Carol froze, blinking up at him, cheeks filling with a telltale blush.

"It's good, right?" she whispered.

"So good," he affirmed, though he hadn't actually tasted the food. "Come with me."

"Where?"

He had no idea about that, either, only that it was suddenly imperative to have her beside him. "Rounds. Have to make sure everything is running before the storm hits."

Her features tensed with sudden anxiety and her hand crept out, palm flat on his abs. "Is it going to be okay, the storm?"

His fingers slid against her waist. "It's going to be okay," he said with authority that reassured them both. Jones wasn't upset about the storm, but he was downright petrified of whatever was happening between him and Carol. Nothing in his life had prepared him to meet a stranger and become swept away by such a range of emotions. But it was going to be okay. Somehow, though at this moment he couldn't say what "okay" looked like, it would be all right. For both of them. He smiled. She smiled, then rested her head on his chest, her ear over his heart. He pressed his free hand over her ear and tipped forward, kissing the top of her sweet-smelling head.

"Ready?" he asked.

She pulled back and looked him in the eye. "I'm ready."

He wondered, as he led the way out of the bungalow, if she was also talking about more than making rounds with him. "Where's Ribs?"

"He went to find Victoria, wanted to ask her something. Spy stuff, maybe." Her gaze roamed the horizon and he tried to frame everything through her lens: hedge misshapen and in need of trim, dangerous crack in walkway, trashcan near overflowing.

"I think a lot about the resort probably needs to change," he blurted.

Carol didn't reply, but she tipped her head, inviting him to continue.

"The little things I didn't notice before, I'm starting to notice now."

This time her smile was self-deprecating. "I'm sorry. I'm paid to be critical and nitpicky. It's a job hazard that I sometimes can't turn off. I never intended to pass it along to you."

"No, I think it's good. Historically I've been content to be a passenger, to let others lead and take command. I've always been that guy, the middleman who comes in and gets the job done. Not the one who does the planning, and not the one who gets the glory. Just 'regular guy.'"

"I don't see you that way," Carol said.

He quirked an eyebrow at her, smiling at her impassioned tone. "Really? And how do you see me, Carol? Pause here, I need to check this generator." They had to stop talking as he performed a test and the massive generator whirred to life. The resort had a maintenance crew, but the backup generators were so vital Jones liked to keep his own eye on them.

Carol stood with her hands pressed to her ears, eyes on the ever-darkening sky above them. The generator stopped its test, leaving unnatural stillness in its wake. Jones and Carol continued in silence that felt intimate instead of oppressive. Jones reached for her hand, clasping it in a friendly gesture. She gave his hand a gentle squeeze of pressure that felt like a little hug of reassurance. He smiled down at her. She smiled up at him. They reached the second generator. Jones paused and faced her.

"You didn't answer," he pointed out.

"I thought it was rhetorical," she said.

"It's very much not. I'd like to know what you see when you look at me." She was looking at him now, eyes warm and bright and brown. He smoothed a hair off her face with his finger, letting it glide gently down her head.

"This feels a little like walking the plank," she said.

"Why?"

"Because you want me to put myself out there, but I can't see if there's a net. I don't know what's waiting on the other side."

"That's fair," he agreed, but he didn't proceed, either. Both of them were waiting for the other to make a move, to take the first step, to strike the first blow. Instinctively Jones knew it should be him. He was, after all, the man. Men were supposed to be strong and brave, to instigate and take the first step. But he didn't think he had ever been more afraid of anything. In comparison to making himself vulnerable in this way, running toward enemy gunfire was a breeze.

"The thing is, Carol…"

"Not the thing again. David, you're either in or you're out. I don't think there's a middle ground here."

"How can you know that when you've never been here before?" he demanded. He felt irritated, the same sort of irritation Carol seemed particularly prone to evoke in him. It was like she opened the lid on his insides and poked around until she received a response.

Maybe it was the same for her because she put her hands on her hips and frowned at him, and it was so cute he wanted to laugh and pick her up and kiss her and shake her and a million unnamed things that bolted through his mind all at once, too jumbled for him to discern. He was the calm sky and she was the lightning bolt, cracking through from nowhere and disturbing the peace. And maybe that was what frustrated him so badly, not Carol herself but her unannounced disturbance of his tranquil ordered world. Did that mean he was old, boring, and settled now? Or had he always been and never realized? Could a guy who ate the same meal every day on repeat actually be called adventurous?

All of a sudden he wanted to step outside the safety net. He wanted to take a chance on life, on love. What he wanted, he most realized, was Carol.

His hands settled on her shoulders. "Carol."

"David," she said, and now she was the one who sounded panicked. She must be able to read his expression, to know what was coming. He opened his mouth to soothe and reassure her and instead felt the cool barrel of a gun press against his temple.

CHAPTER 28

Jones wasn't sure why he felt such a noteworthy lack of fear in that moment. Maybe because he had finally and at last come to a resolution about Carol. Maybe because years of training kicked in and he felt at home in the unprecedented situation. Whatever the reason, as soon as he realized someone had a gun pressed to his head he went perfectly still, minus a few fingers that caressed Carol's face reassuringly.

"It's going to be okay," he told her.

"I know," she said with a quiet confidence that went to his heart. Unlike him Carol had no training or experience in bad guys and weaponry. That meant *her* unprecedented stillness came from her confidence in him and his ability to handle the situation. And if that wasn't a shot of pure adrenaline, he didn't know what was.

"My boss would like a word," said the man with the gun.

"I'm available to conference," Jones said. "Let the woman go."

"So she can run away and tell tales to your two partners? No thank you. Let's go." He had the accent of one of the mainland gangs. When he lowered his weapon enough for Jones to turn, his hunch was confirmed. The man was oversized in the way untrained people often are, with showy muscles that were good for lifting heavy weights but might not hold up to the endurance of hand-to-hand combat. *I bet you routinely skip leg day,* Jones thought. Guys like that always did, focusing more on their bicep and deltoid development than the core muscles that would carry them through an actual conflict or emergency. Jones's muscles weren't as gratuitous, but they would perform well for him, as they always had. They would also give him speed and endurance, something else he thought his new captor probably lacked.

However, he was the one with the gun. After a quick frisk, he removed Jones's gun and tucked it in his waistband. Jones didn't mind because all of his moves suggested he was a rookie, especially the fact that he'd missed the wicked knife in Jones's ankle strap. If he were alone, he would attempt to overthrow him now and end it. But there was Carol to consider, she so small and soft and, frankly, in the way. He had no means of signaling her to get down, to stay back, to find a spot and hide. Knowing Carol, she would want to jump in and help. It would be that sort of help that could get them both killed.

Jones didn't realize his face betrayed his thoughts until she spoke. "Why are you giving me that look?"

"What look?" he asked. The guy with the gun motioned them forward and they began to walk.

"The Carol-is-making-me-crazy look," she said.

"How can you possibly interpret that look?" he said.

"I've seen it a lot," she said.

"Sometimes crazy is good," he said.

"Sometimes it's not," she rejoined.

"I need to know that if I tell you to do something, you'll listen," he said, infusing his tone with extra urgency. This was life or death. He hoped she realized.

She bit her lip, giving him a few pensive blinks. "I'll try."

"What's holding you back?" he asked. Did she not trust him as much as he thought she did?

"The thought that you'll sacrifice yourself to play the hero," she said.

"No, I'm stuffed to the gills with self-preservation," he said and, impossibly, she laughed.

"Let's make a deal."

"No."

She ignored him, of course, and continued speaking. "I swear to do everything you tell me, as long as it's not some heroic attempt to save me by throwing yourself in the line of fire."

He sighed. "Carol, you don't get to set the terms of the bargain. That's not how bargains work."

"Of course it is. Then you come back at me with your terms, and we negotiate," she said.

They reached a black SUV. Their captor motioned them inside, both in the back seat. Immediately Jones's thoughts went to wrecking the vehicle, but, as if in preparation of such an act, the seatbelts had been cut out. If the guy drove as fast as the gangsters usually drove, Jones and Carol would launch like missiles when the big SUV crashed. To add insult to injury, the driver buckled himself and gave the belt a smug little tug as he eyed Jones.

Jones's mind ran through the next option. He could garrote the guy, but that would also have the unfortunate effect of causing a wreck.

Carol's hand rested on his thigh. "Your terms."

He picked up her hand and brought it to his lips. "You do exactly what I tell you to do, and I promise to live long enough to make it worth your while."

She stared at him unblinking one, two, three, four beats. "Okay."

Before Jones could redirect his attention to their captor, the car stopped.

"The docks?" he said. "Isn't that a little cliché for a meeting with a mobster?"

"Not if I'm taking you to a boat," the man replied. He opened the back passenger door, herding them out with a wave of his gun.

"I'm not inclined to get on a boat," Jones said, tone deadly as he calculated Carol's position relative to his and the man's. Currently they made a triangle. Not ideal, but he could work with it.

"Relax," the man replied. "My boss wants me to bring you to him so you can have a little conversation. For now."

"For now?"

"He hasn't decided what to do with you. He wants to *have a conversation.*"

Jones dithered. Take care of the situation now or get on the boat and take care of it later? He was eighty percent certain he could take the guy, but less certain in his ability to protect Carol from the fallout.

The man, once again reading Jones's intent, now put the gun to Carol's temple. "You can get on the boat now and we can have a nice, happy ending, or you can pick up what's left of your girlfriend on the way back."

"I'm going to remember this," Jones warned him.

The man smiled, unpleasantly smug in his larger size. But Jones knew, even if he didn't, that the most powerful things sometimes came in compact packages. He used his gun to motion impatiently toward the waiting boat. Jones helped Carol, catching her when she stumbled into him. The water was becoming unmercifully choppy, the waves agreeing their displeasure with the rumbling sky. Fat plops of rain let loose, smacking their cheeks and lashes. Any hope Jones had of using the weather for cover was dashed when the man ziptied their arms behind their backs and forced them to lie down in the bottom of the wildly pitching boat.

At least they were face to face. Jones stared at her, assessing. She looked mildly alarmed, afraid and alert but not petrified or terrorized. That was good. Fear he could work with; terror he could not.

"How are you holding up?" he asked. The man started the engine. Beneath them the boat vibrated, tickling their ears.

"Feels a little surreal," Carol replied. "Like maybe this is another stop on the danger tour you've arranged for me."

"If I planned it, we'd stop for food," Jones assured her and, impossibly, she laughed. Her nose turned up when she laughed, and her cheek dimpled. Even bedraggled, hogtied, and soaking wet she was adorable. It was a bad situation they were in, but he couldn't stop smiling as he stared at her. She smiled in return. If not for the man with the gun and the bouncing waves, it would have been perfect.

"Best date ever," she said.

He wagged his brows and scooted a little closer. She eased closer and tipped her face but the tightness of the boat, combined with the erratic waves, made it impossible to do more than nestle. Her head rested against his shoulder. He wanted to pull her against him, to hide her away from danger, to keep her safe. It killed him that when he finally admitted how much he wanted to touch her, he was physically bound from doing so.

The boat slid against the dock, bumping wildly with each roiling wave. Two men stood waiting on the dock, their outsized muscles making them appear strangely homogeneous with their original captor. Either they were bulked up on steroids or they all had the same jungle trainer who wasn't a fan of leg day. Jones studied them in silence, filing tidbits for later use. Which one was the leader? Which should he take out first? Who would be the first to run away once he realized Jones was a threat? War was about so much more than fighting and shooting; war was a mind game. Despite the ease with which Jones accessed his emotions, he'd always kept his mind untouched.

The dock swayed unsteadily in the rolling waves. Carol stumbled. Jones struggled against his ropes, "Can you let me go so I can help her?"

The men paused and looked at him, trying to gauge his angle.

"I mean, there are three of you," Jones said, aiming for the *aw, shucks* farm humility that had always served him well. He had no idea if it would translate to this culture, but apparently so because, somewhat amused, they cut his bindings and allowed him to reach for Carol, threading an arm through hers to keep her steady. He gave her arm a squeeze. *I've got this,* he tried to say. She touched her head to his shoulder with a brief little tap. *I know you do.* In all his life he wasn't certain anyone had ever believed in him more than Carol seemed to, and somehow that made everything inside him come alive. He *would* get them out of this unscathed.

The three men herded them toward a metal building, the only one in sight on the tiny island. Jones thought it was some sort of equipment shed, probably used or formerly used by one of the resorts. The double doors opened and the smell of diesel fuel eked out, increasing his suspicion. No equipment lurked inside. Either the shed was no longer in use or everything in it had already been stolen and sold off. Whatever the reason, it was now a lair for the local gang that tended to flow into all abandoned spaces like tiny spiders. Like spiders, the only thing that worked to eradicate them was heavy-handed extermination. Previously Jones had followed the back and forth of law-enforcement vs. gang with a weary sort of halfhearted interest. The gangs were too big, too entrenched, and too well-funded to be hashed out by the locals. A former SEAL and a couple of spies, however...

The old juices began to flow, percolating his adrenaline. He was ready to go, ready for action. He stretched his neck, first one way, and then the other, prepping his body to spring, as soon as the opportunity became available. To his right, Carol did the same, mimicking his stretch like a lion cub copying its predatory mother. It wouldn't do to greet the gang's leader grinning like a love-struck fool, but it was hard to tamp it down. Carol, he knew, would do whatever possible to help him. She would try to have his back, despite the fact that she was tiny and untrained. And now his heart thumped with something more than adrenaline, something that felt a whole lot like love.

A man sat in the center of the oversized shed, holding court in a cheap plastic lawn chair. He couldn't look like any more of a king if he had a crown and scepter. And despite the overt cockiness that radiated off of him, despite the fact that he was positively tiny in comparison to Jones and the three goons, Jones knew this man was the most dangerous of the four because he was the one with the brains and power.

His eyes were beaded and shrewd as they surveyed Jones and Carol.

"The security guard. I was wondering when we'd meet," he said. Jones, Carol, and the three stooges came to a natural halt a couple of feet away.

"Really? I've never given you a thought," Jones replied, though his tone remained civil, almost cheerful. Nothing would be gained from antagonizing the little guy, at least not yet.

The man smiled. "You should have." His accent was more diverse than the goons. They were locals who had been pumped up and grass-fed, opportunistic hired muscle. This man was something else, a calculating vagabond, the sort who always seemed to go where there was the most opportunity for chaos and harm. Jones had been in a lot of tangles. If you pulled the strings long enough and hard enough, they always led back to men like this one.

"Apparently so. I take it you have contacts in my resort."

The man put his hands up in disarming surrender. "I have contacts everywhere. No need to concern yourself."

Jones gave an agreeable little nod. "Probably so. What was will continue to be, despite my involvement. I'm happy to keep a low profile and put in my time." He gave him his best farm-boy smile and Midwestern shrug. "I am curious, though."

"Curiosity can be dangerous," the man replied.

"Not if I don't plan to follow through on it. I just want to know what's so important, what's so urgent that you feel the need to smuggle it in the middle of a storm."

"Smuggle is such an ugly word. I prefer transport," the man said. "And we are in the middle of the ocean." He gestured expansively around them. "It's always storming or about to."

Jones waited him out, staring, silently challenging him to confess. In Jones's experience, men like these had a compulsive need to boast.

"Sometimes people in power have a need. Like any businessman, I like to fulfill it," the man said.

"Is it food?" Carol interjected. The men looked at her, startled, probably surprised she wasn't too cowered to talk. "I bet it's food. Food is the most smuggled thing."

"It's not food," the man said. He seemed slightly annoyed by the suggestion, as if smuggling food was so far beneath him. What was bigger than food, more valuable, more dangerous?

"Drugs?" Carol tried. Again Jones had to smother a laugh, this time because she'd assumed the Gum Lady tone. If her hands were free, they'd be on her hips. And if the smuggler had any sense, he'd stop now. But clearly he had none, because he shook his head and spoke.

"Not drugs. Drugs would be much easier, no feeding required."

Jones lost his smile because suddenly he knew. Animals wouldn't be worth it, not worth kidnapping two Americans and braving a tropical storm. The man stared hard at Jones, and Jones stared hard at the man.

"I see we understand each other," the man said. He glanced at his watch. "I have a boat to catch. And you, well, I believe we'll leave you here as a little insurance policy while we deal with your partners. Rest assured we'll see you later." He stood. Jones stared down at him, disgust and adrenaline mingling into a potent and dangerous combination. The man stared up at him, feet planted in defiance, daring him to make a move. Slowly, his head tipped toward Carol. One wrong move, Jones knew, and they would kill her. With effort, he stepped aside.

Regal and cocky once again, the man swept by him, his goons following like oversized baby ducks. They walked out the door, bending their heads against the sudden lash of wind and rain. A gust of wind caught the door. Two of the goons yanked it until it closed, plunging the shed into darkness.

The only sound left behind was their breathing. Jones stared at the door, calculating, thinking.

Carol edged closer, her arm brushing his. In the suddenly still, stale air, she smelled sweet and fresh, a scent that went to his heart and lingered. "He was talking about people, wasn't he? He's smuggling people," she whispered.

"Yes," Jones rasped. "Probably little girls." Somehow, it was always little girls.

Carol swallowed hard. Like him, she was probably choking on bile. "What are we going to do?" He loved how it wasn't a question. Girls were about to suffer; of course they would do something, anything.

Jones took a breath, held it, and let it out. What he was about to propose was crazy, but it was all he had. He reached into his boot, pulled out the knife, and cut Carol's bindings, rubbing the circulation back into her wrists.

"How well can you swim?"

CHAPTER 29

They stood at the edge of the surf, staring toward a horizon they couldn't see.

"Our island is that way," Jones said, pointing.

Carol said nothing.

"I know because I charted it when I got here," he explained.

She remained mute.

"It's two miles, should take about an hour. That's a fair distance for a moderate swimmer, especially in open ocean, but I'll be right beside you."

Silence.

"I was a SEAL, remember. I can swim for hours, carrying you, if I need to. I won't let you drown. It looks like we're having a pause in the storm, probably the eye. That should give us enough time to get there before things get bad again."

Still she said nothing, staring dazedly out over the ocean. He poked her bicep. "Say something."

She faced him, took a little breath, and said, "Okay."

He blinked at her. "Okay? Just like that?"

"You say this is the way, this is the way. You say I can do it, I can do it. Okay."

"Why?" he asked.

"Why what?"

"Why do you believe in me so much?"

"A better question would be why don't you?" she countered.

"I guess I went from being the designated fat friend, to being the SEAL team's obligatory little brother, to being..." he trailed off. To being what? What was he now? Carol stared up at him, big brown eyes warm and intense and trusting, so trusting. Suddenly everything inverted itself and flipped upside down. He was no longer the chubby kid who had to crack a joke to make everyone feel better. He was the head of security for a massive operation, an accomplished former Navy guy who was about to get them off this island.

He straightened, then thought better of it, put his hands on Carol's shoulders, pulled her close, and kissed her. Her palms pressed to his chest, she tipped forward on her toes and kissed him back. His hand slid to the side of her neck, angling her closer. Her lips were impossibly soft and warm and salty from the nearby ocean spray. Even with the smell of diesel still shimmering around them, he could still pick out her Carol scent, fresh and sweet and bright, a representation of the woman herself, and he never wanted the moment to end.

Carol was the first to break away, unable to support herself on her toes anymore. She settled flat on her feet, breaking the kiss. They blinked at each other, a little shocked and disoriented.

"Well, that was definitive," she said. Her prim tone was such a contrast to the kiss she just gave him that he laughed.

"Yes, now take off your clothes." He reached for his shirt, yanked it off, and tossed it aside.

Carol laughed. "This is some elaborate pickup scheme." She reached for her shirt, but wasn't quite as bold about ripping it off. Pausing, she glanced at the ocean again. "Is it necessary?"

"Yes," Jones declared. Their clothes would add unneeded weight, too risky for such a long swim. He unbuttoned his pants and shimmied out of them, tossing his shoes aside. "We can come back for them. Or I'll send someone."

"Okay," she said, sounding shy. Tentatively, she unbuttoned her shirt. He probably should look away, but he couldn't seem to, especially when she folded the discarded clothes precisely before kneeling to lay them gently in the sand. Then she stood self-consciously before him, now wearing only her bra and underpants. Jones forced himself to give her only a detached once over before turning toward the ocean.

He held out his hand to her. She grasped it, and together they plunged into the surf.

†

*S*EALs were born to swim. When he realized how hard Carol was working, compared to him, he decided to distract her by telling her about their training. She settled into a nice rhythm, dog paddling at a medium pace beside him. Bobbing gently when a rogue wave happened along.

"The guys and I would come back from a mission and then spend the next day in the ocean again," he mused. "Jordan, that's Shimmer's wife, says our skin will dry out if we're not exposed to salt water often enough. I can't say if it's true or not because I haven't been away from the ocean since I joined the navy."

"Do you miss it?" she asked and took a mouthful of water for her efforts.

He had to think about that. Did he? Before this moment he would have said yes. Of course working a soft job as a security guard couldn't match the life he left behind, unsustainable as it had been. On the other hand he had settled into his post-navy life much easier than he thought he would. He *liked* not traveling all the time, liked having a place he knew would still be his place for as long as he chose. "I miss the guys," he confessed. Having Ribs there made him realize how much. "I miss being part of a team. It was an automatic in, a family away from family." On the other hand, they'd picked up where they left off. And they always did. The lack of proximity was hard, but they were still his brothers. Jones glanced at Carol, her face filled with determination as she kept moving forward, foot by foot. It was strange how much being with her filled some piece of him he didn't know was empty, a sort of longing he hadn't realized he possessed. Carol was the tingle in his spine, the hint of something more, of a future stuffed to capacity with possibility.

She caught his inspection and tossed him a smile. "You're barely breaking a sweat over there."

He was swimming at a snail's pace, for her benefit. He'd always been a fast swimmer, even when he was fat. Even before the navy got hold of him and made him part fish. If by himself he would probably set a new PR getting back to shore. He loved to be in the water, to swim, to float, to tread. But somehow this was better, like some sort of baptism. He was leaving the old Jones behind in that shed, the one who couldn't see his worth, the one who saw himself as the easygoing little brother. On land he would become the new Jones, the one who grabbed life by the throat, who did what needed to be done. He would take care of the current situation, and then he and Carol would have a nice, long talk. What he would say during that talk, he couldn't yet say. But he would think of something, he was certain.

"How are you doing? Do you need me to carry you for a bit?"

She shook her head.

"Because I can," he insisted. It was somehow important for her to know he had her back, that he would take care of her, no matter what.

"Maybe…after…we're out you…can carry me around…awhile…" she said, panting a little with the effort.

Clearly it was too much for her to try to talk while swimming, which was a shame because suddenly there was a lot Jones wanted to talk about, to ask her. Namely he wanted to know about the boyfriend. How serious were they? Would she leave the island and go immediately back to Brody? At some unknown point he had started to think of the man as his rival. He didn't realize he was clenching his hands until his palms started to sting. Consciously, he relaxed.

"The thing is, Carol," he began.

She puffed out a labored little laugh. "Not…the thing…again, David."

"Hear me out," he continued. But a fin nearby caught his attention, and then another. "Hold on." He didn't want her to know two sharks were now circling them, but she heard the sudden tension in his voice and looked around. Either she was too winded or too stressed to say anything, but she whimpered.

"They're just curious," he reassured them both. It wasn't the first time he'd been in the water with sharks. Usually they went away. If they moved in for a closer look, Jones would go on the defensive, punching and kicking. Sharks were scarier when you didn't know they were there. If you could keep an eye on them, they could be managed. He flipped onto his back so he could stay vigilant and also have his legs ready to kick a shark nose, if needed. The new watchfulness, combined with the new position, made talking impossible. Carol swam steadily forward like a little trouper. Occasionally Jones flipped around to squint at the sun, chart their progress, and correct their course. Years ago when he had to take so many navigation courses, he never thought he'd need them as a civilian.

After an hour the island came into view. The sharks abandoned their vigil. Jones flipped back onto his stomach as thunder crashed overhead. He had almost forgotten the storm, but now that the eye had passed it came back with a roaring vengeance, tossing the sea into sudden chaos. Carol began to struggle to keep her head up. Jones put his arm around her neck.

"Float," he yelled over the rain that began to beat down on them.

She went immediately limp, surrendering herself to him as he tugged her the last few feet of high waves until he could stand, then he hooked his arm with hers and dragged her.

They collapsed on the surf. Even he was tired after the last few minutes of fighting the current. He lay on his stomach, sucking sand and air, expelling sea. Carol lay on her back, taking jagged breaths, batting her lashes against the rain, shivering hard. Outside the temperature had probably dropped into the seventies, but the punishing rain made it feel arctic. Jones slid his arm around Carol and drew her against him.

"Good job," he said. His mouth pressed against her ear so he wouldn't have to yell. She shivered harder and rolled toward him, kissing him with a shocking amount of pent up passion and emotion. He kissed her back. Lightning flashed, startling them apart.

She pulled away, yelling to be heard. "I guess we'd better find shelter. And clothes."

"Let's not be hasty," Jones replied, smiling when she laughed. She sat up, a hand on his chest, and froze, pointing. He followed the line of her finger and saw a large boat, the goons and their ringmaster from earlier standing beside it on the dock.

Jones knew enough about boats to realize this one was about to leave. Outside the storm raged hard, tossing the vessel to and fro, even as it was moored. Out on open water it would be misery at least and a death sentence at worst. They must be desperate to make their escape if they were willing to risk it. Perhaps Ribs and Victoria were closing in, perhaps the gangsters only thought they were. Whatever the reason, they were about to make their getaway on the ocean with a cargo hold full of precious little innocents. Jones didn't realize he was standing and striding toward the boat until Carol trotted to catch up, tucking her hand in his.

He stopped short, reining in his wild emotions, torn between protecting Carol and protecting the girls on the boat.

"Obviously I'm helping you," she yelled, giving him the Gum Lady hard stare. There was no time to argue with that stare, even if he had a chance of winning. He gave a curt nod. "What's our plan?"

Jones looked at the boat. Planning, his arch nemesis. "To not die?" he tried.

"Good plan, I like it," Carol said. She took a step forward and stopped short, followed by Jones. The leader of the gang, the tiny man, departed the dock, got into a car, and sped away. That meant not only were they *really* getting ready to depart with the girls, but their leader was smart enough not to go with them.

"If I can get on that boat, I can take them out," Jones mused, albeit in a yell.

"Sounds like you need a distraction," Carol yelled back. She straightened her rain-slicked hair and pushed back her shoulders, taking a step forward.

Jones held her back. "What's your plan?"

She patted his chest. "You have your special talents, David, I have mine."

His eyes scraped her up and down. "That's what scares me."

"How much time do you need?" she asked.

"A minute to get on the boat unseen," he said.

"Done and done," she replied and headed off. Jones skulked behind her, keeping to the shadows. It was a risk, and he was tense. They could shoot first and ask questions later, but Carol had trusted him. He would afford her the same level of trust. For a few beats he got caught up watching as she stalked onto the boat like she owned it, seemingly unaware she was still dressed in only her underwear. He was certain he wouldn't be able to hear anything besides gunshots, especially with the raging storm, but the acoustics of the boat made everything inside echo. He could hear, for instance, the sad weeping of children and the guards attempting to hush them with angry words. And then Carol spoke.

"Who is in charge here?" she demanded, and THE TONE had never sounded so imperious. If Jones wasn't so intent on his own task, he would have rubbed his hands together with anticipation and glee.

On the boat everything seemed to come to a complete standstill. Even the girls had stopped their weeping and seemed to be holding their collective breath. A man murmured something. Jones couldn't hear what it was as he scaled the side of the boat, but it sounded confused.

"I don't think you understand," Carol said in answer to whatever it was. "You cannot go. It's impossible. I don't know who you think I am, but I'm here to tell you. I'm from the Board of Departures, and you failed to turn in any of your relevant paperwork for this boat. If you think you can leave the dock before signing the proper paperwork, you are SADLY mistaken."

There was silence again. Jones wasn't certain what it said about the state of modern governance that the only thing men feared more than a man with a gun was a woman with a bureaucratic quagmire from which they might never recover.

One of the captors muttered something else unintelligible. "No, I will not leave, not until I speak to your manager."

Jones couldn't help it, he chuckled. But it was short lived because he could feel it, the mounting tension of a coming conflict. Jones made his way to the engine room, disconnected what needed to be done, and made his way to the storage hold.

"Don't touch me," he heard Carol say, and that was that. There was no need to burst into the room, but he did it anyway, counting the heads of the people he'd need to take down. Four hostiles. *Don't look at the victims,* he reminded himself. At this point they were a distraction. Carol covered them, herding them into a corner and talking to them in soothing tones. If she had her bug-out bag, she'd be doling candy, he knew.

Two of the goons, the original two who took Jones and Carol to the shed island, were armed. The other two were not, probably relying on their even greater size for strength. Life in combat didn't always work out well, especially when everything happened at once, but in this case training and surprise trumped confidence and puffy muscles. Jones broke the arm of the first man, grabbed his gun as it fell, and shot the second armed man in the shoulder, all within thirty seconds of entering the room. The remaining uninjured hostiles piled on him at once, knocking heads with each other in the process. If his teammates were there, someone definitely would have laughed at the loud "CLUNK" they made. As it was, Jones wasn't laughing when one of them jabbed his kidneys and another clocked his jaw.

As he'd thought, they weren't as well trained as they were overly bulked. For a few glorious seconds he backed out of harm's way and let them battle each other in their haste to strike a few blows. And while their punches didn't feel like tickles, neither were they hard enough or skilled enough to be disabling. Unlike Jones's well-placed hits that left the first man retching, the second bent over and gasping.

He stood at the edge of the scrum, panting, assessing the threat, trying to decide what to do next. He needed to get the girls and Carol off the boat before the next threat arrived, one that might be more lethal for all of them.

Too late, though. The threat arrived, more lethal than Jones could handle. Fortunately for him, this one was on his side.

"What's up," Ribs said casually, strolling into the hold with unhurried ease. His eyes fell to the four men in various states of distress. "You didn't save me any? Greedy, Jones."

"I didn't know you were coming," Jones replied. He sounded exasperated, but it was a farce. He was relieved on a level that can only come from being with someone you trusted as much as he trusted his friends. Whatever happened next, Ribs had his back and would cover Carol and the little girls, too.

"When have I ever missed a party this good?" Ribs asked, toeing one of the half-conscious men on the floor. "Victoria and I were taking care of their boss. He's in custody, at least temporarily, until enough money changes hands and he's back out again."

"How'd you find us?" Jones asked, stretching his neck to ease the kinks. Despite stretching beforehand, he was going to be sore tomorrow. What he needed, he realized, was a speed bag. It was way too long since he'd practiced his punches. He was going a little soft, and that was unacceptable.

"Blue," Ribs replied. "He did a little poking around with comms and satelites."

"He always knows how to find the best parties," Jones agreed.

For the first time they let their attention drift to the muddle of humanity in the corner, Carol surrounded by about ten little girls, aged from about four to eight. She hovered over them, henlike. Now that the threat had been neutralized, protective ferocity had morphed to a sad sort of worry.

"Hello, Carol, darling. You're looking good," Ribs said, then took off his shirt and tossed it to her.

"Ribs, always a pleasure. More so now," she added, giving his shirtless form an exaggerated wink as she deftly caught his shirt.

"I love her," Ribs muttered softly, smiling.

So do I, Jones thought. He didn't know how it was possible. He was certain he had much more to learn about her. But somehow in a way he didn't understand, he knew he'd found his person.

The locals arrived, led by Victoria, quite literally. She barreled in front of a bevy of officers who stared behind her a bit stunned, the way men sometimes are when they learn a beautiful woman can not only speak but also wield a weapon. It was clearly her scene, and neither Jones nor Ribs had any desire to divest her of that. In fact it was kind of fun to sit back and watch her bark orders. At last her nastiness had found a productive outlet on a group of fawning policemen who seemed more than happy to do her bidding. Jones and Ribs sat side by side, smiling in amusement, glad they weren't the ones hopping around like bunnies as Victoria alternated between French and English, snapping at underlings to bring her a coffee and precisely two cigarettes, unfiltered.

He was so occupied with the scene, Jones momentarily forgot everything else, including Carol. When he snapped to attention and decided to find her, she was nowhere to be found. He asked everyone, but no one remembered seeing her.

"There was another woman here?" one of the locals asked.

Jones sighed impatiently. Had he ever been that daft, that blinded by the sight of a woman like Victoria? *Yes,* came the ready answer. Well, no more. The blinders were off. Victoria was interesting and complex, but good luck to the man who decided to delve in and start plucking at threads. Jones now understood exactly what he wanted and needed, someone in his lane, someone who matched the soft simplicity of his grandparents' Nebraska farm. If only he could figure out where she went.

Finally, after making his way through the chain of locals, he reached Victoria. "Have you seen Carol?"

"She went away," Victoria replied, waving away the puff of smoke she'd just expelled. Even though it came from her mouth, she seemed to have no patience for it. And neither did she take pleasure in the cigarette, if the way she angrily stubbed it against the wall was any indication. Even the way she did that was alluring, like some sort of ancient muse. Jones could easily get sucked in again, could find himself staring at her, mesmerized, as he tried to figure out what made her tick. He shook his head, willing himself to focus.

"What do you mean away? Where did she go?"

"Away, back to America." Victoria flicked her fingers impatiently in the vague direction of America.

"No," Jones said. "She wouldn't leave without saying goodbye, without talking to me."

Victoria smiled at him with genuine amusement, for the first time. "And why is that? Do you think you are so special? She's a tourist, here today, gone tomorrow. And even if she weren't, what is love? Merely a distraction."

"A distraction from what?" Jones asked.

"Real life," Victoria returned.

"What is real life without love?" Jones countered.

She lit her second cigarette, the amusement in her smile fading to cynicism. "So much easier."

"Come on, I'll help you find Carol," Ribs said, clapping a hand on Jones's shoulder. It worked to break the trance so he could stop staring at the enigma that was Victoria.

"What's her deal?" he asked Ribs after they'd moved out of Victoria's orb.

"She's been wounded by life," Ribs said, sounding grownup and wise for a man currently watching a Shirley Temple video on his phone.

They stepped outside and Jones squinted against the harsh glare of the sun which seemed to be shining brighter now, after the storm, as if it had to make amends for its brief lapse and disappearance from their lives. "Dude, what the heck," he said, shading his eyes with his hand. "You know how creepy it is to watch that after we just rescued a bunch of little girls?"

"It's Charlotte, dummy. It's her dance recital." He faced his phone toward Jones, who didn't know Shimmer and Jordan's daughter well enough to pick her out by sight, but it didn't matter because all the little girls were adorable.

"Did Shimmer send that to you? I thought he was in Egypt."

"He is. Jordan sent it to both of us," Ribs explained. "She keeps me updated, considers herself my tether to real life."

"Huh," Jones replied, only half paying attention. He scanned the horizon, but there were no hints of Carol. "Do you think I'm doing the right thing here? Or should I let this go and move on?"

"Jones, I think if you don't take your shot, you're going to regret it forever. Jump. Smooth the landing later."

"I barely know her," Jones said, heart thumping.

"Sometimes you can see someone through a window and know they are your person, the person you will love for the rest of your life."

His phone chirped with a text. Jones caught sight of his screensaver and squinted. He held out his hand. Ribs placed the phone in it. A picture of Shimmer, Jordan and Ribs stared back at him, Jordan between them, her face upturned toward Shimmer with a smile. Jones noticed the thing he'd overlooked a thousand times before, the way Ribs's smile was trained on Jordan.

He stared at his friend who stared back, daring him to say something.

"Gaines," Jones said, tone serious.

"What?" Ribs replied, tone defiant.

"What did we call you before the shark bite? I can't remember."

Ribs grinned. "Losses. Ribs was an upgrade."

"I've always just been Jones." It bothered him, that. Everyone else got a cool or funny handle. Shimmer, for instance, earned his name when he burned before his wedding and made the supreme mistake of trying to use an abundance of coconut oil to soothe it while on assignment.

"Because, Jonesie, no one ever found anything about you we wanted to make fun of. Now, *David*, go and get your girl."

Jones glanced at Ribs's phone, still in his hand. Jordan's face stared back at him. "Ribs, don't do the same," he replied handing it over.

"Only in my dreams," Ribs replied, tucking his phone in his pocket as they headed for the resort.

CHAPTER 31

After questioning everyone in the resort, they found Carol in the infirmary. The so-called doctor was nowhere in sight, so Jones knocked on her door and let himself in with an, "It's me," by way of introduction.

Carol lay in the lone bed, the sheet pulled over her head.

"What's wrong?" he asked.

"Nothing," she replied, subdued and standoffish.

"You disappeared," he said, with more than a hint of accusation.

"It seemed like everything was well-handled."

"You're in the infirmary," he pointed out.

"I was a little queasy. It's fine. You can go."

"You want me to go?" he asked.

She paused. It was a tiny pause, but it gave him hope. "Yes."

Was there a question in there or was it his imagination. "Yes?"

"Um…yes."

"So you're going back home, back to America, and we're never going to talk," he clarified.

Again with the pause. "I think it's probably for the best."

"Why?"

She shrugged, the sheet on her head hunching up and down. "Obviously it's been a blip."

Jones stared at her, or at the sheet-clad version of her. "Carol, can you take the sheet off? I feel like we're wrapping up an episode of Scooby Doo here."

"No," she said, now sounding like the Gum Lady of his first acquaintance. And that was how Jones knew she was hiding something from him. He went forward and perched on the bed. She shrank back, holding the sheet against her like a security blanket. He reached around her and tugged it off with a swift yank, the breath rushing out of him in a gasp when he caught sight of her face, bright red, blistered, and swollen to three times its usual size.

"Oh, Carol," he breathed.

"I told you I don't do well with the sun," she said, tears leaking slowly down her swollen cheeks. "And now I'm going to freckle."

"I like freckles," he said. Now that he understood the problem, he felt mellow, almost cheerful. Despite her apparent misery, he thought things might be okay. Or, he realized with sudden understanding, maybe it was simply being with Carol that made him feel that way, a key turning in a lock, a feeling of rightness, like somehow everything was as it should be, regardless of outside forces. He picked up the bottle of aloe gel beside the bed, squirted a dollop into his palm, and began using his finger to smooth over her nose and forehead.

"You would," Carol said sullenly. "This is horrible. I'm hideous."

"I'm sorry you're miserable, but you are not hideous."

She tried to quirk an eyebrow at him, but her face was too puffy to allow it.

"Okay, it's not great," he amended. "But it's temporary, and I'm a pretty big fan of the before. And after."

Her lashes fluttered, causing her red-rimmed eyes to water. "Really?"

"Oh, yeah," he said. He smiled. She tried to in return, but her face was too taut. His look turned sympathetic. "This island has not been kind to you."

"It hasn't been all bad," she said. Her fingers inched forward, resting on his leg. He picked up her hand and kissed it, holding it gently in his.

"Yeah?"

She nodded.

"Tell me the good parts," he commanded.

"I ate some good food. I met some nice people."

"Nice, ugh," he wrinkled his nose.

"I was talking about Ribs," she amended.

"Don't forget Victoria," he urged.

"Would that I could," she said, and he laughed.

"Anyone else?"

"The staff needs some tweaking, but there's this one guy…"

"I hope it's not Manny because he's fired," Jones inserted.

She blinked. "Already? But I haven't even turned in my report."

"He was part of the smuggling ring," Jones said. "Which brings me back to you. How are you doing? We had an intense morning."

"I live for intense," she said sincerely. Jones believed her. No one who looked at her would guess how adventurous she was, at heart. Just like no one looking at him would guess the same, from his farm boy image.

"I know you do," he said. "I have something for you."

"You do?" she asked, sounding pleased and surprised.

He reached into his pocket and pulled out a little stack of papers. Carol watched while he unfolded them and smoothed the crinkles with his hand.

"Once upon a time there was this man who hadn't a clue." He handed her the first paper, the drawing he made when he was trying to strategize, the word "Gun?" along with a banana and mango.

"He moved to a tropical island and met a woman." He handed Carol the drawing he'd done of her from the first day they met, her hair matted with gum. He wasn't a gifted artist, but he was adequate enough to make a fair representation of her. Except he kept getting her expression wrong. No matter how hard he'd tried to make her angry, she kept turning out adorable, eyes oversized, nose tipped cartoonishly, lips overly full. It was basically a caricature, and it made her smile.

"He couldn't understand all the feelings she made him feel." The next picture was a collection of emojis he'd drawn.

"But the feeling he kept coming back to was sameness, rightness, *belonging*." The next picture was a key in a lock.

"She traveled the whole world." He gave her a picture of the globe. "And the man thought maybe she was looking for the same thing he was looking for." He gave her a picture of a home. Unknown to her, he'd drawn his grandparents' farmhouse in Nebraska. He hadn't had time to draw more pictures; he'd have to wing it from here.

"Here's the deal, Carol."

"Not the deal again, David," she said, but she was smiling.

"I'm finally going to get it out." He took a bracing breath. "I think I love you, and I think you love me, too. I know it's crazy, but think of it as another adventure, one we'll plunge into together. As for the boyfriend..." He couldn't seem to keep the tension out of his tone at the mention of the other man, the worst fly in the ointment, as far as he was concerned.

"Brody and I broke up."

His heart kicked and turned over. "You did?"

She nodded, still staring at the handful of pictures he'd given her.

"When?"

"Days ago, when I realized I was feeling things for you, things I shouldn't be feeling. It was confusing, and I called him to tell him. We decided it would be better if we took a break."

"A break doesn't sound very permanent," Jones said.

"My head was muddled. I needed to think. Everything has been so crazy—the gang, the storm, the rescue, the swim. We're basically strangers. I barely know you. Moving here, quitting my job, giving up everything for a man I just met would be the most insane thing I could possibly think of."

His heart sank until she closed her hand around the pictures and offered him a smile, as much as she was able.

"Which is why I think it absolutely must be done."

It was what he wanted, and yet he was so surprised when she agreed that he thought he heard her wrong. "What?"

"You gave me stories," she said, clutching them over her heart with both hands.

He blinked, confused by the sudden topic change. "Yes. You deserve all the stories, Carol, all the adventure." His hand stroked her hair. "All the love."

Her lashes fluttered, flicking away the tears. "Yes, David. Yes to everything, yes to you, yes to a new adventure, yes to moving here. Yes to an unknown future in an unknown place. Just yes, so much yes." She clutched his shirt and pulled him to her, wincing when their lips touched. Jones moved lower, bestowing a kiss on her pale neck, seemingly the only part of her that wasn't crispy.

"You're going to make me eat disgusting things, aren't you?" he asked, lips moving against her throat.

"Every day," she replied. "What are the chances the hotel will hire me as its new manager? Because I'm kind of unemployed after this."

"I think I have some sway," he said, pulling back. He pushed some hairs away from her aloe-slicked cheeks. "This is going to be good."

"I think so," she agreed.

"It's crazy how normal this feels," he mused.

"Crazy how crazy it's not," she agreed. Her finger brushed his nose. "By the way, I do love your freckles. And your abs are better than Ribs's. Don't tell him."

"I'll let him continue to linger in his delusions. He needs them," Jones said, fully aware that Ribs was eavesdropping on them.

Outside the door Ribs smiled and pushed away from the wall, glad Jones could get his happily ever after. It gave him hope. Maybe someday...

His phone buzzed with a text. Jordan had copied him on a picture of Nash she sent to Shimmer, a bowl of spaghetti upended on top of his head. He could just make out her hand in the edge of the picture and realized he was staring at it instead of the messy baby.

He shook his head and shoved the phone in his pocket, forcing his thoughts to work and all he needed to do when he returned home.

Work was life, work was safe. It wouldn't always be enough, but for now it was all he had.

Maybe someday, he thought, and headed toward home.

Thank you for reading *The Guest and The Guard,* the twelfth book in the Spies Like Us series. For more books, please check out my website at www.vanessagraybartal.com.

ABOUT THE AUTHOR

Vanessa is a foodie who also loves to write. When she is not trying to find new ways to use sourdough, she likes to troll bakeries and taste test chocolate chip cookies. She lives in rural Ohio with her husband, children, and sheepadoodle. Her life's goal is to fill her books with enough coziness and sunshine to make someone smile. She would love to hear from you, drop her a line on email or facebook.